Exposing the Scars

A. Mitchell

ISBN-13: 978-0615829081

CONTENTS

Index

Dedications:

For my Husband, Jason who supported me through this whole process and made sure to remind me that I have the imagination to complete it. I love you, My Dear.

For my Daughter, Kylie who was the creator of almost all the character names and being so enthusiastic about my writing.

For my Son, Blair who is the sweetest little thing out there. He showed me how to be patient when I was getting a case of "writers block".

For my Parents, Mary & John. You both are the best parents a gal could ask for!

For my sister, Alisha. Your support through all of this has meant the world to me. You are awesome!

I would also like to thank my co-workers, M & L for all the positive feedback and constructive criticism. You Ladies are fantastic!

Prologue

Yea, thou I walk through the valley of the shadow of death, I will fear no evil;
I fear death just as any other person does, but I no longer fear evil, it was him. For I have given him his death.

At eighteen, one is supposed to be starting an exciting new chapter in their lives. College, boyfriends or girlfriends, parties and maybe even a little naughtiness

from time to time, but not for me.

It took one night, after several years of abuse from the

one person who was supposed to be my protector, to

have my life turned upside down. It took being on the

run with a new identity, to find the meaning of what real

love is.

Chapter one

"Oh god, Oh god" I am breathing heavy, my lungs begging for a good deep intake of air. I have to keep moving, I can't stop yet...not yet. The tree branches are like finger nails clawing at my clothing as I run through the woods. I know I have to make it to the creek bed, I will be far enough out of sight once I get there.

I run harder and faster as I see the creek in the near distant. I can smell the murky water already. I don't care how dirty it may be, I desperately needed a drink. As I approach the creek, I throw my bag down next to a fallen tree, landing on a cluster of moss covered pebbles. A rock formation along the creek has gathered a pool of partially clear water, in an instant I am down on my hands and knees. I submerge my whole face into the pool of water and suck up as much water as my stomach will hold. I drink until I cannot take any more in. I sit back up straight and rest by back against the trunk of the broken tree.

Sitting quietly, I watch from afar as the flames grow higher and burn hotter, I can see the plumes of smoke billowing through a clearing in the trees. With the dampness around me, I use it to scrub the blood and gasoline from my hands and face. All I want to do is cry for the loss of the man who was supposed to be my protector, but had turned into someone or something I no longer recognized. Cry for what I thought was the only thing that I could do to escape the madness of it all. But, I will not cry. I mustn't cry, for I had trained myself a long time ago that crying only makes the punishment worse.

The stench from the blood and gas or the knowledge of what I have done has me turning over on my hunches vomiting up the dirty water I drank and what little food I still had left in my stomach. I continue puking until it all turns to yellow bile rising up. The bile burns my throat and nose much like his throat would have if he were still alive when the match was struck. I had no other option, no help had come for me. What I have done, had to be done.

Taking one last look in the direction of the flames, I send up a silent prayer for not him, but myself, praying that I will survive this and one day be able to move on. I stand up and brush the blades of grass off the rear of my pants and hoist my bag on my back. I set out further into the depths of the forest.

My bag doesn't give much stress on my shoulders, I only packed what little items I have that hold very little memories of him. Before running out of the house, I was able to empty out an old tin box filled with the decent saving that I had worked hard for over the years. I never spent any of my earnings unless it was absolutely necessary. I spent the majority of my teenage years scooping soft serve at a small ice cream station, 'Summer Sweets' that stood next to the school. I lived for those days when I saw my name on the work schedule. Work was my escape, my calm before the storm.

Once I reach the coast line I should be far enough away to take a much needed rest. I don't have a plan or a particular destination in mind, I will go as far as my feet will take me and figure things out as I get there.

I continue to walk faster as I hear the sirens blare in the distance, but I will be long gone before they realize what had happened in that home. With any luck the papers will read, "Two perish in fire" but until then, I will have to keep running. If I was given any other choice, I would have been out of that home many years ago.

At eighteen, I just graduated from Oakler High School and had every intention to get as far away from this place as possible. I dreamed of leaving to a faraway land where I would never have to worry about hurting again. Where the people in my life would love me the way they were supposed to. A world where evil no longer existed. Reality smacks me in the face when I realize good may not always triumph over the evil darkness that resides in this world, but at least I have that choice to find my own version of a faraway land now, the terms of this choice have just come with a price that I will have to live with. I need to keep reminding myself that even with the scars I will carry with me, wherever I may end up, I am alive to pay the price. Things could have turned out much different if I would have made the choice to give up, rather than finally standing my ground.

Chapter Two

By early morning, well before dawn I reach the coast line. It was about a two mile walk from Oakler to Maine's coast. I have walked this many times over the past four years. It has always been my safe haven, a place to release my sorrows without fear of punishment. This is where I met Louis.

I was fifteen the first time I met Louis. While sitting on a makeshift bench crying about what was most certainly going to happen upon my return home, I felt a large rough hand gently squeeze my shoulder. Startled, I shrieked and attempted to run away. As I was running, I stumbled over a rock wall that sat about two feet above the ground, cutting my hand wide open. Louis made his way over with much apprehension. He placed his hesitant hand into my uninjured one and helped me to my feet. Louis was a large man. He reminded me of an old lumberjack. Graying beard, wind burned cheeks, but kind brown eyes. He wore a tattered, old wool jacket and pants being held up by suspenders. Without a word, he guided me to a small cabin set back into the tall grass, hidden behind several large trees. I should have bolted then, but there was something kind and understanding about Louis, so I continued to walk along with him. Entering the cabin, I was immediately overwhelmed with the smell of slow cooked, salted meats and vegetables. Fresh bread was sliced on the little table fit for two. He sat me down in the rocker chair that was draped with a brightly knitted blanket and disappeared down the small hallway off the kitchen. I took this time to look at my surrounding. The living room was small, quaint, and filled with warmth. Whether the warmth came from the stoked fire burning, or the presence of Louis, I wasn't sure. But I felt safe here, for the first time in a very long time, I felt safe. Louis had reappeared with antiseptic cream and a bandage. He first cleaned out my wound, then gently medicated and wrapped it.

During that first meeting with Louis, no words were spoken. Over time, it had become a monthly ritual for Louis and I. I talked, he listened. Even though he never spoke more than a few acknowledging words, I felt like I could tell him everything, so I did. It was the summer I turned sixteen, a particularly bad year, I shared my story with Louis.

I can see the faint flicker of a candle burning in the window of Louis's cabin. I make my way to the door and give it a light knock. Louis opens the door for me immediately. Sensing something is wrong, he pulls me through the door. I sit down in the old rickety kitchen chair. While walking, my adrenaline was at an all-time high, but now that I sit and take a breath, I feel overwhelmingly exhausted. Louis places a cup of chamomile tea in front of me on the table. The scent of it relaxes me and the warmth of it eases the chill deep in my bones. I don't know how long we sit there, but finally Louis speaks up.

"Morgan, the time has come hasn't it?"
Closing my eyes and putting my head down, I nod.

I knew coming here was the best option I had, Louis understood what I needed without having to ask. Although he helped by just being a person I could come to, I couldn't stay any longer than necessary. I would not get him involved. He has lived in peace out here for many years, and I intend on keeping it that way. Louis put an afghan and pillow on the ripped, orange couch and left me alone with my thoughts. I must have fallen right to sleep because I barely remember lying down. I awake as the sun was rising over the tree line, desperately trying to erase the images my wandering dreams brought forth in my sleep.

Stifling a yawn, I recall what had happen the day before. With shaky hands, I pull out my sketch pad and pencil and begin to write a farewell letter to Louis:

To my Dearest Friend,

I will be off with the rising of the sun for I have finally had the courage to say no. I will not return, therefore I would like to give you my sincerest thanks for what you have done for me over the past several years. Without your compassion and understanding I do not believe I would have survived. With this letter I leave you with something to remember me. All I ask of you is to remember me as a friend, not a damaged soul.

With all the love I can give,

Morgan

Placing the letter on the table, I set the braided bracelet I made during one of my walks to see Louis on top of it

and headed out the door.

Chapter Three

I made it to Bradford just past nine o'clock.
Bradford is a smaller town, not much bigger than Oakler
but it is the closest place that has a bus station. The bus
station is dimly lit, the florescent lights in the corner
flicker, bulbs pleading to be changed. The rows of plastic
chairs are stretched along the walls and in the center of
the small building. Only a handful of people are sitting
down waiting for either family members to arrive or the
bus itself. I set my bag down on one of the chairs in the
corner and pull my baseball cap down over my eyes,
trying to hide as much of my face as possible. I walk up
to the square, glass window. An older woman who

looked to be in her late sixties looks up at me and

smiles,

"Where to, sweetie?"

The woman's deep, east coast accent came to life

when she spoke.

I hadn't thought about where I was going to go yet,

so I had no destination in mind to give her,

"Umm...Is there any way to get a ticket for a

general location? I'd like to get on the next bus out".

She looks through the papers that are spread

across the desk, then started tapping the keys on the

computer's keyboard,

"Okay, the next bus going out is at eleven and it is

heading south. What you're going to have to do is

purchase new bus tickets at each stop until you figure

out where you want to go. The ticket you buy here will take you as far as Charleston, North Carolina".

Alright, this will work. I'll only have to wait a little over an hour here and hopefully by the time I reach Charleston, I will have an idea of where I want to end up,
"I'll take it. How much?"
I reach into the pocket of my fleece jacket for my wallet. A printer quiets down next to the clerk and she slides the ticket through the open space at the bottom of the window,
"It will be $113.00, please".

I give her the exact amount and take my ticket. I walk to my seat and sit down abruptly, the events from last night and the walk here this morning has me both physically and emotionally drained. I had a fitful sleep at Louis, my dreams playing back yesterday over and over like a movie that was stuck on repeat during a precise horrific scene. But, it could have been much worse, I could still be inside that house with him, reliving not a movie stuck on repeat, but my real life horror flick. I shudder at the thought.

Wind catches the propped open door and slams it shut hard, I jump out of my chair from the loud noise. People turn to stare at me, probably thinking I am some insane girl who has recently escaped from an asylum. Sitting back in my seat with my head down, I have to link my hands together to try and stop the shaking. My mind keeps playing the scene from last night over and over, will I ever be okay with what I did?

A voice over the PA system brings me back into the present. The voice announces the boarding preparations for the bus due for Charleston. Standing up from the chair, I take a deep breath and grab my backpack. We walk in a single file line as we board the bus. I mentally count the number of passengers, hoping I won't have to sit side by side with some random stranger. I glance nervously in front of me, what if someone on here knows who I am and what I've done? I need to stay calm right now, I cannot draw any attention to myself. I pull my hat further down and stare at my feet as we make our way along the isle.

Finding two empty seats in the back of the bus, I collapse down on to it in a heap of exhaustion, my body weary from walking and thoughts of what lie ahead racing through my mind. I wrap my fleece tighter around me, fatigue slowly setting in. It didn't take long for me to drift into a disturbed slumber with the whispers of passengers and traffic on the road fading into the distance.

"Miss, Miss! Wake up. Are you okay?"

Opening my eyes I am face to face with an older, heavy set woman with a Southern drawl hovering over me. Startled, I quickly perk up in my seat, the nightmare all too fresh in my mind,

"I am so sorry if I disturbed you, I must have been having a bad dream".

The woman gave me a soft, concerned smile,

"Oh child, don't be sorry. It sounded like a dream you didn't want to stay in".

She was definitely right about that.

I wipe the tear stained streaks from my face before I stand up to use the restroom. With only two rows of seats between me and the bathroom, I quickly get up and am inside the door in three long strides. I make sure the lock on the door clicks into place before I turn around to see my reflection in the distorted mirror. The dark circles under my steel gray eyes make them look so empty, a look I have become all too familiar with over the last four years. Turning on the cracked, dirty faucet, I cup my hands with water and splash it in my face. I attempt to wash away the grim that has built up on my skin. I tie my hair back in a tight bun at the base of my neck to keep it off my face. Pulling concealer out of my backpack, I smudge it below my eyes to try and hide away the weariness around them and pinch my cheeks to rid them of their paleness. It's the best I can do with what little I brought with me. I take a deep breath, trying to calm my raging nerves. In my mind I am chanting 'I can do this'. I have to do this, I don't have any other choice. My hand rests on the door handle for a moment while I work up the courage to go back out there. Even if this bathroom smells like a football players dirty gym bag, I think I'd rather hide out in here until we get to Charleston.

I walk out the door and make my way back to my seat. I can feel the stares coming from every direction. Do they know what I've done? If they knew the reason, they certainly wouldn't be judging me. I sit down and shake my head, of course they don't know what I did, and they have no clue who I am. They are probably looking at me because I just had a mini melt down while I slept in the seat next to them.

Getting comfortable in my seat again, and trying very hard not to let the stares get to me, I lean my head against the cool glass window and stare out at the passing scenery. An image of a photograph came to mind, a photo of a woman standing at the edge of a look-out point with a big bridge off in the distance. Closing my eyes, I am brought back to the memory from when I was about ten years old.

I waited until my dad was busy outside doing yard work to sneak into his room. He always used to say nosiness was my flaw and if I didn't mind myself, it was going to get me in trouble someday. While I was digging around in his closet I noticed a brown, cardboard box labeled "Junk". I pulled the box down from the back of the closet shelf and brought it over to my dad's bed. The box was full of random knick-knacks that didn't hold any meaning to me and obviously not my father either.

Rummaging through it some more, my fingers ran along a smooth, leather surface. From the outside, it looks like a leather bound book with stained stitching along the binding. The first few pages were covered in drawings, mostly swirling lines and abstract shapes. I continued to turn page after page looking at pictures of flowers and shrubbery, and some of my father posing in front of a silly road sign. Then I came across the picture of the woman and that bridge. The picture was taken from a distance and was quite fuzzy, but I had grown to learn that she was standing before the Golden Gate Bridge in San Francisco. I remember being so lost staring at the photo that I hadn't realized my father had come in to the room until the book was slammed shut and I was being pulled by the arm out of the room. I was given a stern talking to about my snooping and was strictly forbidden from entering his room unless he was accompanying me. He refused to answer any of my questions about the book or the photo of the woman. When my father said, "End of discussion" it was the end of it. But, because of my father's strange reaction to my questions, I had

become that much more curious. Every so often when he

was gone to work, I would sneak back to his room and

search for it. It was nowhere to be found.

I wonder what it is like in San Francisco?

I pick my head up off the window as the thought creeps

in..

I guess I will just have to find out.

Chapter Four

"It's the big Two-One! What's the plan?!"

Avery says to me very loudly, much too early in the

morning.

I have no interest in making my birthday a big

production, but by the big smile on Avery's face, I think

she has other plans for me.

I peek my head out from under the blankets and give her

my best angry morning face,

"Avery... Can you please lower your voice and remove

yourself from my room".

Avery just laughs at my facial expression and climbs on

to the bed with me and snuggles close, she whispers

softly through the covers,

"Is my beautiful birthday girl in a bad, bad mood today?"

I try my best to give her a fake whimper,

"I am not in a bad mood, I just don't want you to go

overboard today, can't we just skip today all together?"

Avery sits up on her knees and starts bouncing like a

five year old,

"MORGAN JAMES! Get your sorry ass up!"

I can't help but smile at Avery, she has been my saving

grace since I came to California. I don't know where or

what I would be doing right now if she hadn't come in to

my life.

I met Avery about three months after I got to San

Francisco. We met at the Fall Festival in the beginning of

September that was being held down by the water's edge, the Golden Gate Bridge and all its glory right there for all to see up close. I was standing there staring at the big, beautiful structure when an arm shot up and looped through mine,

"Stay calm, be cool. Just walk along with me and act like we're having a funny conversation".

This girl on my arm started to laugh out loud and said out of the side of her mouth,

"Laugh with me, pretend that you've known me forever".

I gave her the best laugh I could muster up but it sounded so strained and completely confused.

She started to walk faster, pulling me towards the ferris wheel. She cut a group of kids in line and handed the carney two tickets for each of us. The kids that were behind us started grumbling about us cutting them, but this girl didn't bother to acknowledge them and continued to lead me to the bench seat of the ferris wheel. I looked out in to the crowd and noticed a man frantically looking around for something or someone. I turned my gaze to the girl next to me. I saw that she was looking at the man also. She was slouched down in the seat and had pulled the hood of her thin sweatshirt over her head. She didn't move or say anything until the ride started,

"Phew! That was a close one".

She laughed again and pulled off her hood and sat up straighter.

"Care to explain what the hell that was all about? And maybe who you are?"

"This is what that was all about".

The girl pulled a brown, leather wallet out of the front pocket of her hooded sweatshirt. She opened the wallet and started to count out the bills that were inside of it,

"You stole that!? What were you thinking?!"

She gives me a heavy, irritated sign before responding,

"Yes, I did. That tool deserved it though. If you're going to wear a suit and tie to a carnival, you are just asking to get picked. Who seriously wears that here?"

I was not sure how to respond to her line of thinking, I just knew she had to be bad news and I needed to make my exit fast before she drew attention to not only herself, but to me as well. I could not chance getting picked up by the police and questioned.

The ride finally descended and I was able make a break for it. I waved a quick goodbye to the girl and made my way towards the entrance gate. I could hear footsteps hitting the dirt behind me,

"Hey you! Wait up!"

This girl was going to be the death of me.

"I'm sorry but I have to get going, I have a lot of things to do."

She continued to follow me out of the gate and down the street,

"Like what?"

"Like what, what? And will you stop following me?"

She chuckled and picked up her pace so she was now walking side by side with me,

"You said you have things to do, what would those things be?"

I stopped dead in my tracks,

"Okay, listen. I don't have anything to do, but you are starting to freak me out a little. Don't you have other pockets to pick?"

This girl starts hysterically laughing,

"You are an angry female, aren't you? I like it, I like you.

I'm Avery, by the way".

I looked at her like she was the strangest thing I have

ever encountered,

"I may be angry, but you..you are one strange girl".

I started to walk again when she once again started

following me,

"And you are still following me. Are you lost? Lonely?

You are acting like a stray dog without a home".

"Funny you should say that...Because I am new in town

and I don't have anywhere to stay. Do you know of any

places to rent that are cheap, and I mean, extremely

cheap. Ones that also don't identification or plastic?"

Something the girl said struck me, was she on the run

too? Maybe having someone like her around me would help ease this transition, It couldn't hurt to give it a try, would it?

"Right now I'm staying at the Sunrise Inn. It isn't much, but it's cheap and as long as you pay in cash, they don't ask questions. It's along the water, so that makes up for the smell"

"Sounds so divine!"

I rolled my eyes at Avery. In a weird way, her fake enthusiasm was a breath of fresh air. It was pretty nice talking to someone other than myself.

"So, before I continue to follow a stranger, are you going to tell me your name or do I have to guess?"

Oh shit! Do I tell her my name or make up one? I should have thought of this long before. I should have been prepared for this. I said the first thing that came to mind,

"I don't know yet".

Avery looked at me for a long moment, understanding written all over her face,

"I've always liked the name, Morgan. How does that sound?"

I gave her a wide smile, relief washed over my face,

"Sounds perfect".

Like me, Avery was not from here, she migrated from Arizona. Both of us had a story, but we had an understanding that neither of us needed to share the details. It seemed that I wasn't the only one that wanted to remain invisible.

It didn't take long for Avery to meet some very sketchy people. They seem to flock to her like bees on flowers. One "friend" in particular was an artist like me, so Avery said, when she brought him over the first time. Turns out, Bobbie had a gift of producing excellent fake ID's and providing paperwork that actually looked legit. I will forever be grateful to Bobbie for changing me from Emma Reece to Morgan James, even though I had to sell at least three of my drawing and take money out of my savings to pay for my new name. It was worth every penny I had to spend, I couldn't chance someone finding out that I had resurfaced here in California.

I pull the blanket away from my face, "Avery, I will get up if you would be so kind to get off me".

She rolls her body over mine and lands her feet flat on

the ground,

"Alright, I'm out. But before I leave, what is the first

thing you want to do today to celebrate?"

I wait until I'm clear across the bedroom and into the

bathroom before I give her a grumbling response,

"Avery, I have no interest is doing anything today. I have

to get ready for work, as do you."

I click the bathroom door shut before Avery has a

chance to wallow in her misery about having to actually

do work to make a living instead of reverting back to her

old ways of picking pockets like she used to do when I

met her nearly three years ago.

Once I got my new ID I was able to start looking for a

job. I was hired at a small book store a few blocks from the apartment. After a lot of prompting and I mean a lot of prompting, I was able to convince Avery to also look for work that wouldn't eventually involve me bailing her out of jail.

Avery got hired at the coffee shop across town.

After finishing my shower, I stood in front of the mirror and stared at myself. This is the only time of day that I allow myself to relive the events of that day and every horrible day before that. I see my eyes and I see him. It takes me back to those moments when I wasn't allowed to look away from them. I had to force myself to hold back the tears because I knew what would happen if I cried. To this day, find it impossible to cry without the fear taking hold. I still have only freely cried for Louis and even then, I was terrified he would find out I did. "Get a grip, Morgan" I said with a heavy sigh. Looking away from mirror I finish drying my long, wavy brown hair and pull it back into a pony tail. I was never one to wear much make up but today I take out some rose blush to put some life into my porcelain cheeks and run the bristles of the mascara brush swiftly through my lashes just to add a little boldness. I leave the bathroom in search of my calf–length boots to wear with my skinny jeans and loose–fitted shirt. Even in the summer heat I tend to wear tops that cover my arms and I sometimes find myself pulling the sleeves of my shirts well past the palms of my hands. The marks are no longer visible, but the reminder of the invisible scars run deep within me.

I find my boots and slip them on over my jeans as Avery walks out of her room donned in one of her usual outfits, which I like to refer to them as "costumes". Her sense of style differs from mine on so many levels. Where I tend to be more casual, jeans and tees, Avery decks herself out in fishnet stocking underneath holey jeans, combat boots, and an assortments of lace tops pairs with leather corsets. She likes to think of herself as a clothing artist since her ability to create actual art is non-existent. She once had me try to teach her how to sketch a picture, a tree to be specific. You would think that drawing a tree would be a good, simple start for her..that was not the case. Avery got as far as the middle of the trunk before getting frustrated, breaking the pencil in half and nearly tossing the sketch pad into the pond. That was the end of her art career.

I had started to seriously sketch and paint when I was fourteen as a way of keeping track of what was happening. Where most girls my age had diaries or journals to document their daily activities and boyfriends or breakups, I sketched my days. Drawing moments in my life was a way to remember why I needed to leave, not reminisce at a later time. From the ages of fourteen to eighteen my drawings depicted very disturbing pictures, dark and dangerous sketches of a girl who may not live to see the next day. Now I try to tell a different story. A story of peace and venerability in a life of hiding, friendships, and the thoughts of future possibilities that still lay ahead.

I look at Avery and give her a little snort of laughter, "You do know you have to wear a uniform to work right?"

Avery gives me her standard eye roll and pulls her green "Need Caffeine?" work shirt out of her tote bag, "I refuse to wear this horrifying ensemble until I am inside those doors, but out in public? Absolutely not."

"All right, all right. But remember, we need you income just as much as mine. I do not want to be living back in our old place".

Avery makes a fake puking sound as she shoves her uniform back into her oversized leopard print bag,

"I have lived in many shitholes in my life, but I think that dive takes the cake. Do you remember that dead ground squirrel we found underneath the bathroom cabinet?"

"That had to have been the smelliest, most disgusting thing I have ever seen. AND that is why you need to pull that pretty shirt back out of your bag, put it on, and get your butt to work so we never have to experience that death trap again."

"Whatever, Ms. Bossy Birthday Girl."

"Enough of the birthday comments. I am leaving for work now, and I will see you later this afternoon. But please Avery, nothing extreme tonight."

With a wave goodbye, I walk out of the apartment. I can still hear Avery ranting about her uniform being the least of my worries for what she has planned for tonight.

Chapter Five

Bracken Books is located on a corner lot just three

blocks from our apartment. The red brick exterior has

that beautiful aged look to it, it makes you want to step

back in time when you enter then large blue double

doors. Every time I walk into the store I'm bombarded

with the aroma of dust covered books and fresh coffee,

such an intoxicating mixture.

"Good Morning, Morgan dear. How are you doing

today?"

I look over to the doorway of the office and see Rose

Bracken, the owner of the bookstore standing there

holding two cups of hot coffee in her hands,

"Good Morning to you too, Miss Rose. I'm doing okay

today, how about yourself?"

Miss Rose walks over to me, setting the coffees down on to the front desk and leans in to give me a great big hug,

"Happy Birthday, Dear. I know you have warned Robert and I that you aren't excited about your birthday, but I couldn't resist giving you a good gramma squeeze. Now, take this coffee off and sit back and enjoy it before you open up the store."

"Thank you, Rose."

Miss Rose and her husband, Robert have been so good to me since I started working here. They are like the grandparents you wish upon a star to have. If only I had a chance to know my real grandparents. Rose is a teeny, redheaded woman with freckles to boot. I think she could win any argument with anyone, especially Robert. She has comebacks that would put any comedian to shame and Robert takes it all like a champ, he just looks lovingly at Rose and smiles a big cheeky smile. Robert is a tall, handsome man with salt and pepper thinning hair.

His olive-toned skin makes Roses translucent skin stand out when they are next to each other. I have enjoyed many days listening to their little battles and was amazed at how easily Robert gives in to Rose.

After I finish my cup of coffee from Rose, I immediately get to work opening up the store and setting out this week's "Employee Picks" onto the window display. Rose and I had a rush of customers around lunch time but for the most part it was a very quiet day.

"That is enough for today, Morgan. Why don't you get going because I am sure your friend, Avery is excited for your return."

"Avery can wait, Rose. I don't want to leave you in case things get busy in here."

"Now, child. Who do you think ran this store before you came along? I did perfectly fine then and I will do fine now."

Miss Rose grabs my shoulder bag from behind the register and leads us to the door. I attempt to turn back around to protest, when she winks and gives me a soft kick to my behind.

"Fine, fine. I will leave, unwillingly I might add. But I will be making up the extra hours on Monday."

With a tight hug, and a kiss on the cheek to make up for the kick to the butt, I wave goodbye to Miss Rose.

It was just before three o'clock when Miss Rose shooed me out the door to start my birthday celebrations early. She was adamant that she was fine with taking care of the customers and closing up.

As I stand outside the big, blue double doors of the Bookstore I am welcomed by the bright hot sun and blue skies that is only shaded by a few feathery clouds. Its always such a joy to walk past children running through sprinklers in their backyards or toddlers slurping on sticky popsicles while the parents try desperately to keep it from dripping on to their brand new summer jumper. I had always looked forward to summer as a child, when there was no school to wake up for or books to finish reading before the next book report was due in Mrs. Jones' class. The endless hours of fun, only returning home when my father or the babysitter's voice became hoarse from yelling my name at dinner time. Those are the days I wish I could keep front and center in my mind, rather than the days that came all too soon, that inevitably closed out any hope of a continued childhood.

Instead of going home right away and dealing with the shenanigans Avery is conjuring up, I decide to head across the street to a little art gallery in hopes of showing a few of my newer sketches and checking out some of the newer pieces that were being advertised in the flyer at the bookstore.

Frost Gallery was modern compared to the old-fashioned businesses around it. They upgraded the basic red brick to gray and tan stones with steel trim around the edges that glistened from the sunlight. Bay windows covered every inch of the building where stone didn't touch, allowing pedestrians to take a glance without having to step foot inside. I, on the other hand, could not wait to get inside to see all the displays set out, hoping that one day my work could be up there as well.

"Good afternoon, how are you enjoying the pieces?"

A small, stout man in slacks and dress shirt said from behind me.

I was admiring a beautiful painting that captured the essence of movement within it. The waves looked as if they were coming alive with avid force to crash against the rocks.

"It's a very enthralling piece. Is the artist local?"

The man walked behind his desk and returned with a detailed slip of paper in his hands,

"This picture was done by a painter out of San Diego, but we have many local artist that show their items here."

With that in mind, I decided to go for it,

"Would you be willing to take a look at some of my work and tell me what you think?"

I held my breath and waited for his response, making myself lightheaded for how long he had me wait for an answer.

"If you have things with you, you can leave it with me, otherwise feel free to bring it back in. I don't have time to look through it at the moment but within the next few weeks I can hopefully give you an answer or at least an opinion."

With as much excitement I could possibly muster without looking like a desperate lunatic, I squeal in excitement.

"Oh that would be fantastic! I have most of my recent work with me. Take all the time you need to look them over."

"Just leave your portfolio and contact information next to my desk and I will be in touch. If you have any questions just call or stop by and ask for me, George Froth"

I thanked George several times before returning to the

amazing pieces of magic around me. If only one day, I could have something on these walls.

I take my time getting home because I know Avery is going to be in an eager mood to go out and celebrate my new legal status. I figure it won't hurt to give her this night since I make it a point not to go out very often like she always wants me to. I am not one with the night, or night-life I should say. Actually, if you were to ask Avery she would tell you that I don't care to venture out at all unless it is within walking distance of our apartment.

I walk into the apartment, surprised she hasn't filled the place with balloons and confetti, but extremely glad she hasn't. I head straight to my bedroom to prepare myself for the night out, and with Avery that can only mean insanity of some sort.

I decided to go all out tonight. Rather than keeping my

hair pulled back like usual, I let my long wavy locks flow freely down my back, curly the ends to make whimsical wisps. Adding a touch of mascara to my long, thick lashes, the blackness to the eyelashes make my already big gray eyes seem so much more alluring. I pull my long, slender legs through a pair of black leather pants that Avery forced me to buy at the thrift shop where we do most of our shopping, and a silver tunic tank top with flecks of gold speckled along the hem line. I pair the outfit with some simple black pumps that will do doubt cause aching feet by the end of the night. I don't dare look at myself in the mirror, there is no changing my mind about tonight.

I walk out of my room, avoiding eye contact with Avery. All I can hear coming out of her bright red lips is cat calls and whistles.

"Holy hell MJ, you look like a sex goddess!"

Avery hops off the island and hugs me tight, clearly
proud of my clothing accomplishment.

"Stop it. Can we just get going before I change my mind
about this whole night."

Taking a deep breath to calm my nerves, I guide Avery
and myself out the door and in the direction of Corner
Cove Pub.

When we get close to Corner Cove we notice several
people crowded around the front of the pub. At closer
inspection, two guys are getting pulled apart by a large
man in a black "Security"
T-Shirt. The security guy is holding on to the back of an
obviously, beyond drunk guy. A woman is standing off
to the side screaming obscenities to the bouncer and
begging to let him go with her. A car pulls up in front of
the building, the woman opens the back door and
steeples her hand in an awkward attempt to convince

the bouncer to get the stumbling drunk into the car with her. Mr. Security drags the man by his shirt and tosses him in the car, giving fair warning to the woman that he is no longer permitted into the Cove. I glance over and notice Avery has her eyes locked on the other guy involved in the altercation. Since I have known her, she always seems to be drawn to the bad boy kind. I look back to the divided crowd and have to do a double take. There, standing directly across for me, a flock of woman being the only thing that separated us, has to be the most handsome man I have seen. He has to stand at least six and half feet tall, which would easily tower of my five feet seven inches. I wish I could get a better look at his eyes, but they are shadowed by the lamp hanging on the corner of the street. If I am not mistaken, it seems that he has noticed me as well. The butterflies in my stomach are fluttering like crazy, I have never been in a situation like this before. I don't know whether to look away or keep staring and oh boy to I want to keep staring.

"Earth to Morgan..."

"Huh? What did you say?"

"I asked if you were ready to get inside and have some fun because the people out here have obviously started without us."

I watch as the man from across the way walked in to the Corner Cover, excited rushes through me at the possibility of seeing him again once we get inside.

Turning to Avery, we both look at each other and a big smile breaks out onto Avery's face.

"This is so exciting! What a great start to a great night!"

With a roll of my eyes, I grab Avery's hand and make my way through the still lingering people. We finally make it inside the front door and we don't even make it to the bar when someone is shoved hard into me from behind. Like a game of dominos, I'm then smashed into a rock hard surface. As, I step back to get my barring's straight I realize the hard surface I hit was the back side of one beautiful, male specimen, the same man from outside.

The saying you hear all too often; Tall, Dark, and Handsome only begins to describe the man that is standing in front of me. Dark shaven hair with day old growth on his chiseled, square jaw. His ice blue eyes shine as bright as the blue sky on a hot, cloudless day, eyes I so badly wanted to see just moments ago. Even with his simple black t shirt, the contours of his well-defined muscles are easy to make out, not bulging muscles seen in the gym or on the cover of body building magazines, but clean-cut, toned muscles. He raises one arm, rubbing the back of his head and I can't help but notice the bared skin along his waist that is exposed when he raised his arm. Part of a tattoo possibly? How amazing it would be to get a closer look. Oh my, what am I thinking, I have never been this fixated on a man ever. Avery is the man-lover, I am the one that usually runs in the opposite direction if ever approached by a man. I can't find it in me to look away from him, his eyes have me locked in and I realize that he is looking at me just as intently, both being held captive by the other. I look deeper into his eyes, committing the blue shade to memory, when he gives me a soft, shy smile that shows off a dimple on his left cheek. I have just swooned that much more. I can feel the red hot heat making its way up my neck, towards my face, the blush of ten women in a hot sauna. Recognition flashes in his eyes, although I can guarantee we have never met, he isn't someone you could even think about forgetting. He opens his mouth to speak when I am forcefully grabbed by Avery and pulled to the bar. I look back to see my mystery man is no longer there.

"We are here for a celebration and you take off and hide on me"

"Sorry. I was...I don't know what I was"

Avery gives me an exasperated huff and raises her hand to get the attention of the bartender. She orders two shots of tequila and two tap beers to start the night off. I think I am going to need a lot more to drink if I want to try and get that man out of my head.

"Hey Avery, did you see where that guy that I fell into went?"

Avery just giggles and gives me a knowing look.

"No, and why are we wondering where he disappeared to?"

I can't look her in the eye when I answer because she will know I am lying, she is too smart for her own good and she also knows me well enough to know that I would never concern myself with a man unless there is good reason.

"I just want to apologize and make sure he knows it wasn't intentional."

I inwardly cringed at how desperate I sound, it is completely out of character for me to be this interested in someone, especially someone I haven't even technically met. I have steered clear of any type of relationship, boyfriend or friend since I was fourteen. The closest thing to a relationship I have not is with Avery and before her, it was just Louis.

I'm starting to get sticky from all the dancing we are doing. My long, thick hair that was once nicely curled, is now stuck to the back of my neck in tangled dampness. I can feel the alcohol running through by veins, taking over my ability to think coherently it makes me feel invincible and so much alive. I raise my hands higher in the air and bounce to the music, not caring that I cannot dance a lick to save my life. I sway my hips from side to side on the dance floor with Avery, wondering what it would be like to have a man's hands holding tightly to my hips, a man who wants to hold me because he loves me, not a man who's only goal is to hurt me inside and out.

As these proclamations go through my mind I am reminded of why I came to San Francisco in the first place. I need to remember to be cautious and leery of who I get involved with. I can't afford to make any mistakes or I will find myself on the run again and leaving Avery is not something I want to do.

My shoe prediction came to life in full force, I slip off my heels and make my way back to the bar stool and order myself another shot of tequila, taking is straight–no chaser needed for tonight. I sit back and watch Avery effortlessly grind herself in between two men. Her long blonde hair is damp and tangled together from the heat of all the bodies around her. I watch in awe as she can so easily let go of whatever brought her here, and how she owns her own happiness. Realization struck me, I need to start taking a cues from Avery and just throw my head back and tell universe to go fuck itself.

A middle-aged man comes out from behind the bar carrying a brightly lit birthday cake. I look over to Avery with her glossed over eyes and big smile, I can't be angry with her, so instead I take another shot the bartender placed in front of me and give her a big hug.

The party goers around us start to sing "Happy Birthday" to me but I easily tune them out when the striking man from earlier re-emerges, the crowd dividing giving me a clear view of him, much like Moses raising his arms to create a path through the water. With his arms crossed it front of him, he stands there watching me...watch him.

The singing appears to have ended and Avery is yelling for me to blow out the candles on top the cake. It has been years since I had candles to blow out, so I close my eyes and really take the time to make a wish. I thought about all the times in my life back home when I closed my eyes and prayed for wishes to come true, but they never had. Maybe this time will be different. I could only think of one thing that I wanted to come true more than anything...healing. I want to wake up one day and be fine. Be fine with what I had to endure throughout the years, be fine with what I had done to escape that torture, and just be fine with the person I hope to become. I open my eyes wide and take a deep breath, blowing out the candles. I manage to blow out most of the twenty-one candles on my own but with some help from Avery, we blew the rest of them out. Cheers and whistles erupted around us, making my ever-charming blush to creep back up.

Warm air brushed the back of my neck and worked its way up to the side of my face. A soft voice whispered into my ear,

"Would the birthday girl be so kind to accept a kiss from a stranger?"

My breath catches in my throat as I turn around to see the breathtaking man that watched me from afar. His eyes bore into me as if he can see into the depth of my soul. This mystery man slowly leans in and brushes his soft lips across my cheek and stops just shy of my mouth. I want to turn into the kiss but I am too shocked to move. I am taken aback by the effect this man has on me. My insides warm to his closeness and has me feeling weak in the knees.

My voice finally comes back to, I am able to squeak out a simple hello. I try to focus on what he is saying but my eyes are busy gazing over the rest of his glorious physique.

"I'm sorry, what did you say?"

I bring my hand to my ear in an attempt to play it off that I didn't hear him because of the noise, not because of my inability to stop staring at the rest of him.

"I asked you for your name, I'm Jack".

The way his eyebrows slightly raise after having to repeat the question, I knew then that I was busted and I am pretty sure he liked that I was enjoying his closeness.

"It's nice to meet you Jack, I'm Morgan".

Jack places my hand in his and brought them to his lips. He gave a soft, simple kiss to my knuckles. The desire that shot through me in that moment was completely unexpected, warmth pooled in the pit of my stomach, working its way even lower as he held my hand. Jack slips my arm in the crook of his and guides me to the dance floor. He places my hands behind his neck, my forearms resting on his perfectly wide shoulders. The more we dance, the closer we get, and the lower his hands travel. His long fingers skim just underneath the top of my leather pants underneath my tank top at the small of my back. Breathing heavily, I have to pull away, the touch of his hands on my skin has my head spinning.

"I have to go, I need air, I...I need air"

Stammering my rushed words, I bolt towards the exit sign with Jack following close behind.

"Morgan, Wait. I'll come out there with you."

"No, Jack. Please. I promise I'm fine, I just need a few minutes alone."

Jack stops and stares after me, confusion written all over his face.

Falling back against the side of the building, I try to take big gulps of air. I don't know if I am shivering from the cool breeze an impending storm is bringing or from how hyped up my body feels. The pulsing heat in between my legs is slowly subsiding, but the butterflies in my stomach are ever-present.

I stay with my hands covering my face for several minutes until I can feel myself gaining back some of the control I had lost with Jack. I look around at the city lights that are becoming obscured by the wall of fog, wondering if I should head back inside or just go home for the night. I know Avery will understand if I decided to leave, and with the way I was acting with Jack inside, I don't think I can trust myself to make good judgment calls right now.

I walk back to the door and peak my head in. Avery is leaning over the bar fanning her face and giving her best sultry smile, I can only assume she is trying to earn herself some free drinks or offering the tatted up bartender and endless night of fun. Turning back outside, I shake my head in amusement. She has the ability to have any man fall all over her. I cannot count the men that Avery has wrangled over the last couple years of knowing her, but she has yet to ask one to stick around. Avery firmly believes she is just weeding through the bad ones until Mr. Right comes along.

Chapter Six

I wake to my mind still reeling from my encounter with the mystery man, Jack but the smell of fresh brewed coffee eases my mind and just thinking of the warm liquid running through my dry throat gets me up on my feet and following the scent. I make my way into the kitchen and take a seat in the high-back stool at the island. Avery hands me a large cup of blacker than black coffee, just the way I like it; strong. I pick it up with both hands and bring it close to my face. I inhale deep through my nose then take a sip, closing my eyes and savoring the taste of it. Avery puts her elbows on the counter with a questioning look on her face and slides a folded piece of paper in front of me. I must have had a confused look on my face because Avery came around

the island, putting her arm around me.

"The guy you danced with last night gave me this when I

was getting ready to leave. He wanted me to make sure

you got it right away this morning."

I unfold the paper and read it over and over before

handing it to Avery to look at.

"MEET ME AT DOLORES PARK TODAY AT NOON, I WOULD LIKE TO

SEE YOU AGAIN. I'LL BRING LUNCH"

-JACK

"Wow."

"I know. What should I do?"

My palms instantly become moist at the thought of

meeting him.

"What was the first thing that came to mind when you

read this?"

I peek over to Avery with blushed cheeks and a light
laughter in my tone.

"I don't think I should repeat the thoughts that are going
on in my head right now."

Avery lets out a loud snort and claps her hands together,

"Well, you have three hours to make a decision. If it were
me, I'd go. But you need to do or don't do this for
yourself."

"Can't you just make the decision for me? Or better yet,
come with me."

What would Jack think if I showed up with backup?

"I am not coming with you to meet up with the first man
you have ever acknowledged. Just take your cell with you
and I can check up on you. We could have a code word
just in case things are going south."

"That is actually a good idea. We can use...red...like
"Code Red"."

Avery slaps her hands to the counter laughing hard, making me jump out of my seat and splatter my coffee. "Oh my god, Morgan. You are too funny. Red it is, then."

"Now I just need to figure out how to act. Just the thought of meeting up with his has my stomach in knots. Why me?"

"Why not you? You are beautiful, smart, funny when you let yourself relax. Any man would be lucky to have you on his arm. Just be yourself and if he doesn't like who you really are, then screw em'."

"Thank Av. You always know what to say when I am about to have a nervous breakdown."

"Likewise. I figured I owe you since you are always there to talk me out of my many 'manly'mistakes."

I couldn't help but laugh at Avery's word use for her many almost one night stands. I couldn't understand many of her choices with men she planned to sleep with.

"So, Morgan. I have to ask this....How did you sleep last night?"

I thought about the question for a minute, realizing how refreshed I felt. I didn't have dark puffy circles under my eyes or congestion from crying while I slept.

"Actually, Avery...I feel great. I feel like I had the best sleep of my life. I don't remember the last time I slept that good."

"I didn't hear you at all last night, so I am assuming you were terror free. I am not going to ask you what they are even about, because I know you won't talk about it, but I am just glad you had at least one night away from them."

"Yeah...Maybe they will be gone for good because I could use more nights of sleep like this one."

Jack...

I lay back on my bed replaying the night with Morgan
over and over. I can't quite figure her out, usually it
takes me just looking at someone and they're an open
book. I can't get over her eyes, so mesmerizing, but also
so sad. Normally when I am hired by a client to locate
someone, I do my job and not ask questions. But
something about this job makes me want to find out
more. Why would he have to hire me to look for her, and
why is she trying so hard to stay hidden?
I never meant to go that far, I just wanted to get a closer
look at her. But the moment my lips touched her I was
completely spellbound. The feel of her skin on my
fingertips had me wanting more. I had to remind myself

that she was the objective here, not someone I could get involved with, but the instant she withdrew herself from my grasp and ran out the door, I felt cold and alone. Her warmth was stripped from my body and I wanted it back. I'm not certain if it was for the job at hand or just wanting to be near her again that possessed me to give a note to the girl she came there with, I am not one to go chasing after some girl, but then again, I can't shake the feeling that Morgan isn't just 'some girl'. A tightness in my chest formed at the thought of her not showing up and rejecting me.

With an old photo of a girl that appeared to be Morgan in my hands, I picked up my phone and dialed his number.

"Hello"

"It's Jack, I think I may have found her."

Hanging up the phone, I get that same feeling I got the first time and I spoke with this man...dread. He says she's a runaway, but most people who have a child that has run away deal with the police, like my parents did when my sister, Sarah when she ran away, not a PI, we are usually there last chance stop. He gave me specific demands, the main being no police involvement. Every-time he calls the first thing that comes out of his mouth is, "Did you find that girl yet!"...not... "oh, please tell me you found my daughter". There is so much distain in his voice when he says 'that girl'. I have a sickening feeling there is more to this than just a runaway daughter.

With my elbowing holding me, I look upwards, staring up into the sky. An outline of a woman shields my face from the bright sun, I quickly sit up realizing its Morgan standing over me. Elation comes over me, I can hardly contain my surprise.

"You came."

I give her one of my biggest smiles. The smile isn't fake, I am truly excited she actually showed.

I watch as she runs her teeth across her bottom lip, wanting so badly for those lips to be on me instead.

"I almost didn't, and I'm not exactly sure why I did. Why did you ask me here anyways?"

"Because I really wanted to see you again. You left so abruptly last night, we really didn't get a chance to talk at all."

I gesture for her to sit down next to me, but instead she sits on the furthest part of the blanket as possible. She seems a little nervous, almost skittish today.

"So, Morgan No Last Name-what's your story?"

I meant for the question to be funny, to loosen her up a bit, but the look she shot me had me wondering what her story actually was.

"There is no story to tell, nothing spectacular here."

Morgan made sure to respond in a way that told me to not push it or she's out before this day even got started.

"I'm sorry, did I say or do something wrong? In all honesty, I would just like to get to know you more."

I reach into the cooler I brought along and pulled out two sandwiches and water.

"I told you I would bring lunch, so...turkey or ham?" Holding out both sandwiches for her to choose.

"Turkey. And thank you for lunch, it was very thoughtful."

Morgan grabs the bottled water and turkey sandwich, slowly unwrapping it. After a brief moment of silence, she finally speaks up.

"Well, I live with my friend Avery downtown, not too far from the Corner Cove actually. I work at the Bracken Book Store, and that's really it for me. What about yourself, Jack No Last Name"

I have to laugh at her for throwing that comment back at me. I see she can be witty when she wants to be. I just realized I am going to have to bend the truth with her, about my employment anyways.

"Well, let's see here, I've only lived here a short time and I live by myself in a closet sized apartment near Chinatown, and I work in...ahh...freelance."

I throw that word out much louder than it needed to be, which has Morgan looking at me like I've lost my mind.

"And what do you "freelance" exactly?"

Morgan gives me a nervous look, not sure if she can trust me... if she only knew that she is the object of my freelancing.

Thinking on my toes was never a strong suit of mine, I have always been a man of honesty but this is a different circumstance, so I manage to answer her with some truth to make me feel better about the white lie.

"Photography"

Morgan gives me a small nod that seems like an approval of my response.

I decide to dig a little deeper and try to get the background story as to why I am even looking for this woman, or if it's even her at all.

"So, what's your family like, did you grow up here in San Francisco?"

The reaction I got from her was not expected, if she was a runaway like he made it seem, why did it look like she wanted to cry and run for the hills?

Morgan stood up quickly from where she was sitting and looked away from me,

"I'm so sorry, but I have to...I have to leave...I need to leave."

"Morgan, Wait!"

She started walking away from me, almost into a jog. I caught up with her and grabbed her arm. The way she cowered down and covered her face with her hands, you would think she was a beaten dog. I immediately removed my hand from her arm and raised them out to my side in surrender. I couldn't leave it like this, I needed to know more, I needed...no I wanted...to know her.

"Why do you keep running away from me? Whatever I said or did, can we please rewind it and act as if it never happened because obviously something did".

I bob and weave my head up and down, side to side, trying to get her to look at my face, but Morgan refused to look at me when she eventually speaks.

"Look, Jack. I am sorry but I have a lot of things going on right now. I don't think this is going to work. I should have never come."

"There has to be some way to make you stay and talk to me. I just want to get to know you."

"I want to get to know you too...but if we are going to do this again, I have one condition."

Morgan finally makes eyes contact with me, waiting for me to comply.

"Anything, just name it."

"We don't talk about our lives...before we met. Or at least my life before we met."

For any other person that would seem like a strange request, but knowing there has to be some important reason, it makes enough sense for me to agree. I can't help but find myself more excited about spending time with Morgan than actually doing the job at hand. Reaching out my hand in truce and agreement, I grasp hers and shake it soft, but firmly.

"It's a deal."

"I love this park, even with all the people around, it's always so peaceful."

I watch as Morgan lazily looks around at her surroundings. Her long, brown hair is lightly blowing in the wind, and her pale shoulders are becoming pink from the sun. I have never seen such a beautiful, yet innocent woman before. Yes, I have had my fair share of beautiful women, but nothing like Morgan. Just the watching her close her eyes and breathe in the afternoon air has me adjusting myself like a fourteen year old boy seeing a hustler magazine for the first time. In a flash, I knew I was in trouble, a kind I have never experienced before. One look at her big, piercing gray eyes last night and it was over for me. I could look into her eyes every day and be happy with my life. I didn't have to know her to know what I felt when I first laid eyes on her, and then to feel her skin, it was like a knockout punch. I felt the sudden urge to capture this moment, never wanting to forget Morgan's face tilted to the sky with her lips turned up into a small smile.

Click

"What are you doing?"

"I'm sorry...I couldn't resist, you looked so beautiful."

A tide of crimson washed over her face at my words.

"You are very charming, you know that?"

"I try."

Morgan let out a cute little snorted laugh and I just couldn't resist taking one more picture of her like that.

Her laughter caused a light swell in my chest. I wanted so badly to reach out and pull her close to me, but I knew it was too soon and I needed to be careful with this one.

Lunch soon turned in to dinner, and before we knew it then sun was setting over the bay and I was forced to say goodbye to Morgan.

"Are you sure you can't stay out a little longer?"

"No, I can't, I have to open up the store tomorrow. But, thank you for today. It was very nice, I don't think I had that much fun just sitting around...so thank you, Jack."

"I had a great time too, Morgan. Is it too presumptuous for me to ask to do this again, soon?"

"I would like that very much."

I can't get the day with Morgan out of my mind, like she said, we didn't do anything spectacular. We sat or walked and talked around the park. Morgan wouldn't even let me take her someplace nice to eat, we ended up grabbing chili-cheese dogs and shared cotton candy from a sidewalk vendor. Everything about today was simple and easy. I was so happy and scared, I didn't know what to do. Reaching for my phone on the coffee table, I decided I needed to talk to my dad.

"Hey, Son"

"Hey, Dad"

"Uh-oh. Something is wrong. What's going on Jack?"

I can hear my mom in the background asking my dad what is wrong with her 'baby boy'. I think my mother has forgotten that I am twenty-five now and not five.

"I met someone."

"Ahhh...Women troubles, this I can help with."

"It's not really troubles exactly. I just met her and I can't stop thinking about her. I feel like I'm going to lose my mind if I don't see her soon and I just left her."

"Son, its obvious you like this girl. And what you're feeling is completely normal with us Sloan men. Do you remember me telling you about how I met your mother."

"Yeah, Dad. I remember. You knew you were going to marry her the moment you met her. I remember the story."

"Then you should understand that what you're going through is exactly what I went through."

"If it was just that, it would be fine, great in fact. But when she finds out what I am really doing here, I don't think she will care to be around me."

"Wait, what would it matter why your there...unless..."

"Yeah...She's the girl I am supposed to find for that guy in Maine."

"Oh dear."

"Uh–huh...So, what do I do?"

"Honesty. That's the only answer I can give you. Your Mother and I raised you kids to be honest, no matter the cost. And if this is meant to be, she will forgive you."

Talking with my dad usually made me feel more certain about things, but not this time. I knew I needed to tell her the truth, but I don't think I am ready to lose her yet.

I think it is about time I rethink this 'runaway girl' job, that way I won't have to lie to Morgan anymore because I will no longer be looking for her.

Chapter Seven

It has been nearly a week since I spent the afternoon
with Jack at the park. My days went by in a hazy blur
with the busy work days and helping Avery battle a three
day hangover which she swore was just the flu, but
seeing her stumble in early Monday morning with only
half her clothes on, told me otherwise. Because of all the
craziness this week I hadn't the chance to see Jack again,
but a few late night talks on the phone makes me eager
to put his face to that seductive voice. While talking for
more than an hour last night, I agreed to meet Jack
tonight and with it being a Friday, I had no worries of an
early Saturday morning. I decided to ask Avery to come
along to help to ease my nerves.

With Avery and her friend, Cole in toe, we all make our way into the Hatch House Bar. Walking in, I am instantly bombarded with the smell of spilt beer not completely cleaned up from the night before. The dim lighting showcases the oak bar stretching along the length of the room. I spot Jack leaning against the back wall near the pool tables, the baseball cap he's wearing shields his crystal clear blue eyes from my gaze. I take hold of Avery's hand and make my way towards him, not wanting to wait another second to be near him. Spotting my approach, Jack pushes off the wall with his foot and starts to walk towards us. Avery lets go of my hand as I meet Jack halfway.

"Hi"

My voice is shaky with nerves and excitement. Jacks returns a hello, smiling at me as if it was the happiest moment of his day. I can't help but feel both nervous and relaxed at the same time when I'm near him. He does something to me that I can't quite explain.

"How was your day today? I hope your week got better, mine is certainly ending on an excellent note."

There is that smirk I have become very fond of again. "It must have been the storm we had this week, everyone stocking up on books while they were stuck indoors. But now that the work week is over, I hope to enjoy my weekend."

"If I can help in any way with that, just say the word." My infamous blush creeps back in at Jack's flirtatious remark, my insides are giddy with anticipation of what this could mean for me. What if I can't go through with this…whatever this may be? What if everything turns out to be just the same as it was back home, I refuse to let that ever happen again. Before I can think on this any longer, Jack takes my hand and leads us to where Avery and Cole are setting up the table for a game of pool.

"Hey guys, I have someone I would like you to meet. Avery and Cole…this is Jack. Jack, this is my roommate and current best friend, unless she wakes up with another week long hang over, Avery and her friend,

Cole"

Jack shakes Cole's hand and gives Avery a light peck on

the cheek.

"It is nice to meet the both of you. Now, how about a

game of pool to start the evening."

Avery is definitely a pool shark and ultimately suggests

a battle of the sexes, to say I was a little disappointed is

accurate. The image of Jack wrapping his arms around

me in an attempt to coach me on holding the stick

properly is something I would not be able to pass up. It

looks like I may have to suggest a 'couples'game next

round.

Racking the balls, Avery bends down over the table with

her sun-faded too-short shorts, looking straight into the

eyes of a man sitting in the corner watching her every

move and smashes the queue ball, never taking her eyes

off him. She lands two solids into the pockets and set

herself up perfectly for the next shot. She goes at for a couple more hits before finally missing, giving the men an opportunity to come back. I stand off to the side awaiting my turn while Jack is staring intently at the table. His brows are furrowed together, deep in competitive concentration. He walks around and stands in front of me, leaning over, he aims his shot. Perfect shot into the left corner pocket, he turns around and smiles at me. I'm lost in the moment of his closeness, I can smell subtle cologne, Irish Spring bar soap, and a hint of sweet from the whiskey he is drinking. The smell of Jack is intoxicating, and so painstakingly heavenly.

Jack slowly brings his hand to my face and gently brushes away a hair that has fallen from behind my ear, I can't help but lean into his tender touch. His warm hand sends a shiver through by body, igniting a feeling I am not familiar with. All I want to do at this point, is leave this bar and have Jack wrap those hands all around me and never let me go.

Avery clears her throat to get our attention, Jack and I both look up and realize there is no gap between our bodies and everyone in the bar seems to be staring directly at us. Jack clears his throat and smirks while I take a step away from him. Excusing myself, I go straight into the restroom to calm myself down.

Holding the porcelain sink tight with both hands, I try to rein in my emotions. What has come over me..I think I might be losing my mind. Maybe I'm not ready for someone like Jack, just yet. I should just end whatever this is now before it becomes too much for me to handle.

Avery softly knocks on the door before pushing it open and coming in.

"You need to explain to me what just happened out there with this Jack guy"

I close my eyes and grip on to the sink even harder, feeling myself fade at just the mention of his name...I have it bad.

"I wish someone would explain it to me too because I have no idea".

Avery shoots me a look, clearly just as confused as I am.

"What exactly do you mean?"

"What I mean is, I have never had feelings like this before, or even remotely close to what I feel when I'm around him. I have only been around him on three different occasions and each time the desire for him gets stronger. I just don't know what I should do. Should I end it now before it gets to serious? Or just wait it out?" My body is tingling at just the thought of going back out there and being so close to him that I don't know if I will be able to control my temptation to touch him or hold him. Every time I look at him all I want to do is run my nails across his back as he whispers my name sweetly in my ear. I would even be satisfied to just feel his lips brush upon my mouth.

Avery turns away from the mirror after reapplying her deep red lipstick and looks at me, about to give me her best attempt at womanly advice.

"I get that this scares the shit out of you, hell anyone can see that. Take my advice and go for it, don't think so much and finally have some fun for once! Maybe this guy is your practice run to dating or he might just be your Mr.Right."

"I thought Mr. Right was all yours."

"Well, Jack can be your version of Mr.Right"

We both laugh in unison, making my nerves ease up a bit.

Taking one last deep breath I pull open the bathroom door, smiling back at Avery, thankful to have her in my life.

"Ok, I can do this."

Jack and Cole are sitting at the bar when we leave the restroom, pool sticks put back against the wall, having what seems like a comical conversation. Cole is gesturing wildly with his hands and arms while retelling one of his dramatic tales of his latest excursion. Cole is what you would call a "Free Spirit", never a dull moment when he is around. Cole is one of Avery's closest friends and possibly the only man she hasn't slept with this side of the Golden Gate Bridge. Cole is notorious for telling outlandish stories of what he has seen or done across the world. Cole was born and raised in San Francisco and comes from a lot of money. Cole's father split when he was just a baby, but his mom easily bounced back and ended up marrying his father's best friend, who is possibly one of the wealthiest men in San Fran. Cole's Mom, Candi set him up quite well with a condo along the beach, an expense account I will never earn in a lifetime and encouraged him to live the life of an avid traveler until he 'found himself'. Even with all his lavish luxuries, he still remains down-to-earth, funny as hell, and a loyal friend. When I met him the first time he was dressed head-to-toe in basic khaki and unshaven. You would have never guessed he was just returning from a month-long trip to Egypt because he was getting bored with the California scene and needed to get away. From the way he presents himself, I would never have

expected him to be one of San Fran wealthiest,

unattainable bachelors until Avery told me otherwise. He

is the complete opposite of some of the other wealthier

individuals in the area. But, Avery loves him to the ends

of earth, so I must tolerate him, with much ease.

With a nudge from Avery, I take a seat in the stool next

to Jack. Avery sits down by Cole, conveniently cutting

off his storytelling. Jack turns his body around on the

stool away from Cole, and gives me his award–winning

smile.

"What would you say if I asked you to leave here and

take a walk with me?"

I can tell by the hopeful look in his eyes that he really

would like me to say yes. Even though he plays it off like

its fine either way. I decide to make him sweat it out for

a minute.

"Where would we go if I were to say yes?"

Jacks rests his arm on the back of my stool, thinking on it.

"How about we go down the street for some coffee or tea? Theirs is this little Bistro not too far away."

This man has found my weakness...coffee. I look away from his eyes, playfully pretending to think about whether or not I want to go with him. I didn't want to show how badly I wanted to go with him, anywhere with him. He could ask me to go dumpster diving and I would probably say yes. But, before I even have a chance to answer Jack, Avery speaks up for me.

"Jack, she would love to go with you. Cole and I are heading out anyways."

Cole looks utterly confused and opens his mouth to speak, but Avery gives him a hard glare that clearly sends the message to keep his mouth shut. I just sit there, holding back my snicker. Watching them two interact so easily is something I would love to have with a man, even a male friend, hopefully someday soon I'll have that.

"Well...Jack, I guess you have your answer."

With a skip in his step, Jack is off his stool and holding his hand out to help me off mine. Avery walks up and gives me a reassuring good luck hug, she leans close to my ear whispering, "Just have fun, don't worry about anything other than how you feel tonight". After one last tight hug, she and Cole walk out of the bar without a backwards glance.

The moment Avery and Cole are out of sight I immediately get nervous butterflies in my stomach, having no clue what to do with a man at this point. I have spent the majority of my teenage and adult years staying away from these situations, always avoiding the possibility of what would be coming to me if I deviated away from the rule, the rules that were so engrained in my mind. I don't know how to act or really even what to say, but I do know that I want to go with him and for reasons I don't quite understand, I feel safer with him than I have ever felt with anyone else.

We fill ourselves with raspberry glazed croissants and samples of specialty coffees, making simple small talk. I no longer feel awkward or as nervous as I was before. Jack has a way of making me feel comfortable and alive. "Morgan, I know you said we can't ask questions about where we come from or anything from before we met...but what about the general questions?"

"What kind of general questions?"

"Like...What's your favorite color?"

I can't help but laugh.

"Is that something you seriously want to know?"

"Of course."

"Ok...I don't have an exact favorite color, but I do like purple even If I don't wear it that often. What about you? What's your favorite color?"

"I would have to say...as a man...blue of course."

"Just because you're a man doesn't mean you can't like purple too."

"You are a funny gal, Morgan."

It was silent for a moment, Jack contemplating what to ask next. Given my previous rules, I'm sure it's not easy coming up with questions to get to know each other. I just can't risk anything right now. If I give too much away, Jack may eventually figure out what I did or someone might come looking for me.

Jacks looks at me and smiles. Looks like I have stumped him, my turn to ask the questions.

"I know this question pertains to life before we met, but do you have any siblings?"

The smile leaves Jacks face on the spot, I immediately regret my question.

"I'm sorry if I said something wrong."

"You didn't say anything wrong, I was just taken aback with that question. It's still hard."

"I'm not following you, Jack."

"I'm an only child now. My little sister died a few years ago."

"Oh Jack, I am so very sorry. I shouldn't have asked that. I just thought I was being selfish by not giving us an opportunity to know the little stuff. I'm so sorry."

"No, no...it's okay. You didn't know. But, it's a part of me that I would like you to know about. I don't think tonight is the best night to talk about it though. Not great conversation for a first real date."

"Okay. I understand."

I excuse myself from our little corner table, giving Jack a few minutes to himself, and check in with Avery. I wanted to make sure she knew there wouldn't be any 'Code Red' messages tonight. Despite what just happened, tonight has been a very good night.

Jack and I walk in the direction my apartment, subtly bumping shoulders against each other, feel the heated friction every time they make contact. We walk in a comfortable silence, lightly brushing the outside of our hands against one another, but not having the courage to link them together. Sensing by the chemistry between us, neither of us wants the night to end. With the entrance of my apartment fast approaching, we start to slow our pace trying to prolong the end our night.

"I need to tell you something that I should have said right away, Morgan."

"What is it..?"

Jack looks down at his feet, lost in the thought of whatever it is he needs to tell me.

"Uh...Never mind. It can wait until later."

Whatever it is, mustn't be that important, or it is and he just isn't ready to tell me. I know how that feels, there are so many things that I should be telling Jack, but I can only imagine what he would think of me if he knew the truth...if he knew what I did to escape my old life.

"Okay. You can tell me some other time, if you feel you need to."

There was a chill to the air and the stars were shining through the break in clouds. Jack stops me outside my apartment and places his index finger under my chin and raises my head so I am looking directly into his eyes. My breath caught as he leaned his head towards mine. It felt like eternity before his lips connected with mine. He pulled away too soon and looked back at me with a smile. He lowered his lips again and this time I opened my mouth for him, allowing his tongue to gently massage mine. He moved his mouth over mine in a steady rhythm. His lips were like silk, compelling me to wrap deeper around them. Jack pulled his lips from mine again but this time he gave a soft kiss to my forehead causing me to close my eyes and melt into his supporting arms. I wished so badly that I was ready for something more to happen with Jack. I wanted to hang on to him as tight as I could and drag him up to the apartment. With my luck, I would get him all the way inside and have an Oscar winning panic attack, scaring him off for good. This is all so new to me, these fresh, amazing feelings for a man I barely know has me scared, but charged. I want to bottle this feeling up and save it for a rainy day. I just need to give it time, give him chance to prove to me what kind of man he is.

Chapter Eight

It was a smoldering hot July day in San Fran so we had decided to take a drive up to Big Sur and spend the day swimming at the "Gorge". We were already getting overheated just packing up Cole's yellow Jeep with the cooler and lawn chairs, it had to be at least eighty degrees and it was only nine in the morning. The day before, Avery and I had been miserable working in the heat and made a plan to spend the day wading in the cool waters of the Sur River. I was so nervous about spending the whole day with Jack in nothing but a bathing suit, I was making myself sick over it. I wasn't sure if I could do this, I couldn't even make up my mind on what to wear today, and I am not the type of person to spend more than ten minutes getting ready for anything.

This morning I stood in my room with a blue one-piece bathing suit and a black string bikini laying out on my bed in front of me. I couldn't decide which one would be better to wear in front of Jack. Was I ready to show him this much of myself? But I didn't want to seem like a prude either by wearing the one-piece. Avery, the saint, came in to my room to see what was taking me so long and knew right away what my predicament was. She picked up the blue one-piece, scrunching her face, making gag noises and threw it back onto the top shelf of my closet and walked back to my bed and picked up the almost nothing bikini, holding it out for me to put on.

"Decision made. You will wear this one because you are twenty-one years old with a body most women would kill for. So Honey, show off whatcha got!"

With an uneasy laugh, I took the bikini out of her hands and nudged her out the door.

"Okay, okay. But if this turns out bad I am blaming you".

Avery snickered as she walked out my door.

"Yeah, Sure."

There was a knock on the door and I could hear Avery talking to someone that could only be Jack, Cole had already gotten here this morning with fresh iced coffees and poppy seed muffins. Footsteps came down the hallway and Avery peeked her head into my room to see me standing in front of my mirror nearly hyperventilating. I was standing there staring at myself in the black bikini with gold clasps that hooked along my hips. The triangle string top barely covered my round C-Cup breasts.

"Oh wow, you look fantastic Morg! I knew that was the right suit for you."

"Thanks Avery, are you sure it is a good idea to wear this? I don't want to look like I'm trying too much. I promise you I'm not, I just don't want to look like a fool."

"Believe me, Jack is going to be swooning over you when he sees you in that."

"Oh gosh, Avery. I don't want him swooning. Wait, do I?"
"Yes, you most certainly do. It gives us woman more control."

Laughing at Avery, I backed away from the mirror and pulled on my faded jean shorts and a loose fitted racer back tank top.
Jack and Cole where outside finishing packing up the jeep when I walked out of me room. I made a quick beeline for the bathroom to add a little lotion to my legs and pull my hair up into a messy bun to keep it off my already moist skin. It was too hot out to worry about

putting on any make up since it would be washed off from either the water at the Gorge or from the humidity in the air. My natural look will have to just do for today.

Avery and I grabbed the rest of our things and headed out the door. Walking to the Jeep, Jack opens and pulls the seat forward so I can get in, holding out his hand to help me in. As soon as our hands touched, I once again get a tingling shock run through me. I look up into his dark, intense eyes and give him a soft smile. By the way Jack looks down at our linked hands, I know I'm not the only one of us that feels this connection.

Once I am securely in the back of the jeep, Jack climbs in and sits down in the seat next to me. With everyone in the Jeep, we start our two and a half hour trip to Big Sur.

Avery and Cole are sitting up front in a heated debate about who knows what while Jack and I are in back, silent. I can't help but feel his gaze on me and I don't dare look over. I'm afraid if I do, I will get lost in his eyes and be gone forever. With the sides taken down from the jeep, the breeze casts Jack's manly scent all around me, it has me feeling weak already and I could only imagine what looking at him would do.

Avery fidgets with the radio and stops at REO Speedwagon "I Can't Fight This Feeling Anymore" and I can see Avery trying to hold back her laugh as she looks at me through the visor mirror she has pulled down. I try my best to give her an evil look, knowing exactly what she is trying to do. She thinks she's quite funny, using my awkwardness as a way to amuse herself.

My palm flexes flat against the seat and accidently rubs along Jack's tensed, fisted hand. At the same time, Jack and I look down at our hands and then back up to each other. He smiles softly at me, allowing me to release the breath I have been holding them moment our hands touched. He uncurls his hand and gently places it on top of mine, intertwining our fingers. Still staring at him, my heart is beating rapidly in my chest, it rings loudly in my eyes, completely drowning out the music playing throughout the car. It amazes me, how attracted I am to Jack. Yes, he's a beautiful man and anyone with eyes could see that, but this attraction runs so deep. His beauty doesn't seem to be just on the surface, every time I'm near him I feel this incredible pull that I have never experienced before and even with knowing him only a short while I can't wrap my mind around how safe I feel with him. It's like he is making everything bad that could happen, disappear. Even my nightmares have vanished, I hadn't dreamt about that monster since the night before I first met Jack. That has to mean something.

We must have been staring at each other for quite some time, not wanting to break the moment, we were brought out of our mutual trance by Cole's voice announcing our arrival to Big Sur.

The walk up the river wasn't as difficult with Jack walking alongside me. I gripped his hand like it was my only life line and he held mine like he would never let me go. At first, I felt bad hanging on to him while trying to gracefully walk around the rocky terrain, but even with his arm full of supplies, he never let go of my hand. A little ways ahead, Avery and Cole stopped at the spot where the falls flow into a swimming hole. Avery and Cole wasted no time turning and yelling to us to get a move on it.

"Hurry up you two! We're here and it looks like we have the place to ourselves for now."

We continued the short trek hand in hand to where they we standing. We all take in the beautiful sight before us. We have stopped at the bottom on a smaller waterfall that flows into a crystal clear pool of water. The sun is shining through the shades of the trees making the water sparkle like diamonds set into a wedding band. The mist blowing in the breeze from the waterfall hits my skin, sending an inviting chill through me.

Jack speaks almost to himself, still looking out towards the water, hypnotized by the beauty.

"This is so amazing, it's worth the two and a half hour drive."

"I know. It's still just as breathtaking now as it was the first time Avery took me out here last year."

Avery and I got started setting up our spot, spreading out the beach blanket across a large flat rock big enough for all four of us to sit or lay down on. We set up the chairs and cooler off to the side, but close enough to grab what we needed without have to move away from the comforts of the blanket.

Avery was the first to strip out of her shorts and tank. Her short, tiny frame looked gorgeous in her bright red halter bikini. Cole's eyes were glued to Avery's body as she sat back down and pulled her platinum blonde hair over her shoulder, securing it in a loose braid. I had my suspicions about Cole having feelings for Avery and seeing the way he is watching her, has confirmed them. Whether it is emotional or physical feelings, I don't know. Only time will tell. It would be so nice to see Avery get involved in someone that isn't just in it for a quick night of fun, someone like Cole who can make her happy every day even when they are knee deep in heated debates.

Jack walks over to where we are sitting and slips off his leather flip flops. Grabbing the hem of his plain white t-shirt, Jack lifts it over his head, exposing the tattoo that I've been dying to see since the first night I met him when I got a small glimpse of it. It was some kind of tribal tattoo that started half way up his left side and ran down along his ribs. The tattoo continued down beyond his swim trunks where I could no longer see. He also had another smaller tattoo above his left breast, over his heart. Unable to make out what it says, I move my eyes away from his markings to admire the rest of him. I waste no time taking in his glorious chest and stomach.

Jack has nice broad shoulder that went well with his well-defined, lean stomach. His lightly tanned skin glistened with sweat as the sun beat down on his body. It took everything in me to not stand up next to him and run my hands along his moist chest. I could picture myself tracing the tips of my fingers down his tattoo and finding out where exactly it ended. I had to fan myself from the heat that visual brought on.

Jack tosses his shirt on to the chair and looks at me.

"Want to cool off in the water with me? It looks so refreshing".

"Okay. I am getting pretty hot and we did come here to swim".

If he only knew how hot I actually was, and it mostly wasn't from the heat of the sun.

Reaching his hands out to me, Jack helps me up on to my feet. It's the moment of truth as I slid my shorts down then pull my tank top over my head. I don't even

have my tank completely out of my hand when I hear
Jack take a deep intake of breath. I quickly look down at
myself think I must have some kind of wardrobe
malfunction when Jack speaks,

"Oh, wow. Morgan you look amazing. I mean, of course
you look amazing, you always do. But, Wow".

Jack is stammering and stuttering on his words, I can't
help but blush.
"Um. Thanks Jack".

"Let's get into the water before I make a bigger fool of
myself more than I already have".

I laugh and take his hand once again. Looking back at
Avery she smiles and winks at me.
"Told you it was a right decision".

Jack and I wade through the clear water talking about nothing in particular when Cole and Avery come up behind us, bringing a tidal wave of splashes with them. It turned into an all-out water fight, turning the guys against the girls. Splashing and dunking and diving under to escape. I just reached the surface of the water after diving under when Jack's strong arms wrapped around my waist. I tensed for only a moment before turning in his arms. We both stopped laughing as we gazed into each other's eyes. I slowly reached my arms up and put them behind his neck. Not saying a word, Jack lifts my legs and wraps them up around his hips. Leisurely, he carries me to the base of the waterfall that shields us from prying eyes.

With my back is pressed against the smooth rock wall, Jack leans in closer to me and rest his forehead against mine.

"Morgan, I'm going to kiss you now. If you don't want me to, just say so."

I can't even think straight, let alone speak. Jack takes one hand from my waist and brings it to my face, cupping my cheek and stroking it with the pad of his thumb. He brings his lips to mine. The tension that had built up between us all morning didn't allow this kiss to be soft or gentle like our first kiss was. This kiss is hard and hungry, neither one of us was able to get close enough. Jack is devouring my mouth with his, sweeping his tongue along mine, hoping to savor the taste. I almost whimper when he pulls his mouth away, but was quickly rewarded when I felt his tongue run down the vein on the side of my neck. I rest my head back against the rocks to give Jack better access. I can feel a pulsing heat between my thighs where Jack's hardness rests, the large ripples from the waterfall is causing me to slowly rub along his length. Lost in our own euphoria, we don't notice the arrival of swimmers.

A high pitched scream behind us brings Jack and I out of our carnal bubble. Pulling apart reluctantly, I look at Jack who is wearing a lazy smile on his face, just as delighted as I am.

"It sounds like we no longer have this spot to ourselves, we should head back out there with Avery and Cole".

Jack voice is throaty as he adjusts himself.

"You're probably right, Even if that's the last thing I want to do right now."

"Me either."

A small chuckle escapes me as I watch him trying desperately to fix himself and swim after me at the same time.

"Wait!"

Jack catches up with me, he grabs my arm and pulls me back to him.

"Yeah?"

Jack pulls me back into his arms and kisses me sweetly on the lips, then my nose, and finally on my forehead.

My eyes close as he whispers into my ear.

"I just needed one more".

The sun was starting to set by the time we packed up the Jeep and were on the road heading back to San Francisco. I had fallen asleep fairly quickly with my head resting on Jack's lap while he traced little circles along my shoulder.

"Morgan, wake up. Babe, were here".
"Huh?"
Not wanting to move from the comfortable place I was in, I held on tighter.
I could feel something moving gently underneath me, realizing it was Jack's body I was sprawled across, I shot up quick.
"I'm so sorry! I didn't mean to fall asleep on you like that".
Jack just smiles a bright smile at me.

"Don't be sorry, I enjoyed every minute of it. If it was up to me I would have had Cole drive around all night if it meant I could have you this close to me longer".

Avery chose that very moment to chime in, she seems to enjoy embarrassing me.
"Okay, you two lovers. Get up and out and help unload this stuff. Cole has to get going".
Groaning in disapproval, Jack and I slide out of the car to help Cole and Avery.

With everything unloaded and put away, we said our goodbyes to Cole, who was off to jet-set with his mother and step-dad in the morning. If I recall, they were taking a family vacation to Morocco. What a life he lives.

Not ready to have Jack leave, I decided to make a bold move. Something I have never done or asked of someone before.

"So, Jack. Would you care to come up for a little while. Maybe watch a movie or just relax for a bit?"

Jack seemed surprised by my request, knowing by now forwardness is not my strong suit.

"Yeah, I'd like that."

Not thinking this thing through very well, I had forgotten the only televisions in our dinky apartment were in our bedrooms. Nervousness crept back in at the thought of having Jack in my room, on my bed. In all my years, I have never willingly invited a man into my bedroom. Before thinking on it too much longer, I escorted Jack to an island chair and pulled down a bottle of cheap whiskey, pouring us both a glass. I don't drink hard liquor often, but I needed something to take the edge off. Taking a large gulp, the amber liquid burned all the way down to the pit of my stomach.

Jack smirked as he leisurely sipped on his drink.

"Nervous?"

I choked a bit at both the whiskey and his comment.

"Is it that obvious?"

"A bit. I can go if you want."

There was no use in sending him away now. I've made it this far, I might as well see how far I can go before having myself one of my notorious panic attacks.

"No, I'm fine...This is fine...I'm sorry, I'm just not used to having men over. I'm a little out of practice."

Now, that was an understatement of the century.

"That's good to know."

Avery came out of her room freshly showered and dressed to the nines in a skin-tight zebra print skirt, a black sheer tank, and my black pumps.

"I'm out. I'll try to be quiet when I come home...but no guarantees."

"Wait, what? Where are you going? You're leaving? But...But we have company.."

"You have company, my dear Morgan. I, on the other hand, have a date with whoever decides to buy my drinks tonight."

"Um...right...ok."

Oh dammit to all hell. What am I going to do now, Avery was supposed to be a buffer for me...even if she didn't know it. Okay, I can do this...It'll be fine, just fine...ah shit.

Slamming one more glass of whiskey, once again enjoying the burn of liquid courage, I lead Jack to my room.

"I'm sorry, I swear I'm not a total head case."

Jacks laughed as he follows close behind.

"You're fine, I promise. I think it's cute how nervous you are."

Opening the door to my bedroom and flicking on the light switch, I quickly look around making sure I don't have anything embarrassing out for Jack to see. Standing back against my bed, I watch as Jack peruses around. I watch as he touches the surface of my dresser, then my nightstand, my bed, and finally he stands in front of me. Jack stares in my gray eyes for what seems like an eternity before speaking a word.

"Why do I always feel the need to ask your permission to kiss you?"

"I don't know? Why do you?"

"Not sure...But, if it's okay...I'd like to kiss you again."

"Permission granted."

The kiss started off soft and simple, a little peck here and there, but before I knew what was happening, the kiss became a force of nature and in an instant, I was laying with my head against the pillows, Jack lying next to me with his mouth freely roaming over my lips and neck.

Staring into Jack's blue eyes as he lay over me not moving, I could drown myself deep into those ocean blue eyes. The heat between my legs is building, it don't know if I can handle much more of this, without taking myself to a place that I'm not sure I'm ready for.

Jack brushes a loose hair away from my face, then pushes himself up to his knees.

"I think I need to stop before I'm unable to stop anymore."

As good as Jack was making me feel, I sigh in relief.

"That's probably a good idea."

"How about that movie instead? I think I need something to distract me from how amazing you look right now."

My hands shoot straight to my face in an effort to cover my blush. Jack is the first man to compliment me and not expect anything in return.

"A movie sounds good, throw in whatever you want. Everything is stacked on top of my dresser."

Jacks picks a movie at random, puts it in the dvd player and comes to sit back next to me back against the headboard.

"Hey Jack, can I ask you something? If you don't want to tell me that's fine."

"Ask away"

"How did your sister die?"

Jack stares at the television for a moment, clearing his throat, he turns his body to me.

"Car accident...I'd like to blame the guy she took off with but the accident wasn't his fault, just her running away was."

"What do you mean...ran off?"

"My sister met a guy when she was seventeen, the guy was bad news. Once they realized things were getting serious between them, she was forbidden to see him again. My parents were never ones to pick and choose who we dated, but there was just something about this guy that didn't sit right with them. He was rude to them, he didn't care what I, as her older brother thought, and I swear he was abusive to her. Not physically, but I don't think he has too many kind words. Even with all that, my sister was still in love. She was seventeen, how could she really know. Then, one night, she was just gone...left a letter to my parents on her bed saying she'd be in touch once she and Luke got settled. Three months later my parents got the call. A semi cross the median, hitting my sister and Luke head on. There were no survivors, my sister and Luke went fast, felt no pain. The driver of the semi had a heart attack, which caused the accident."

"Oh, Jack. I so sorry."

"Thanks. It's still hard to think about Sarah being gone, but we're all dealing."

After Jack's confession, the night slipped into an easy companionship. We kept our hands to ourselves for the most part, a small kiss here or there and subtle touches that never went too far. Once Jack went home for the night, the sexual tension between us had built to an all-time, I was almost tempted to take matters into my own hands...literally.

What am I going to do about that man?

Chapter Nine

Jack..

Weeks went by in an endless blur of picnics in the parks, go-karting, dancing and dinners, just making our mark on the city together. I've been on an all-time high whenever I know I get to spend time with Morgan, even if it's only for an hour, or a minute. I have never felt this alive in my whole entire life.

My life has always seemed good and easy. A family that loves me and my sister, Sarah unconditionally. My parents made sure Sarah and I never wanted for anything. They never missed a sporting event, a gymnastics competition, or even a spelling bee. Although my parents didn't care for my career choice, they understood why I felt the need to do what I did. At first, this PI stuff was just a hobby to make extra cash in college; girls wanting proof that their boyfriends were cheating on them, or proof of professors sleeping with their students. Things became a lot more serious the moment my sister became a runaway. It took me three months of using every trick in the book from lying to stealing to threats of permanent damage to get close to the whereabouts of my sister. But by that time, my parents were already getting the bad news of her death. When the man looking for Morgan called, I jumped right into the job. My parents had to wait three months for an answer, I couldn't image what it felt for this man to have to wait three years for any answer at all. Now that Morgan knew the story of my sister, she will understand my reasons for looking for her at first. But, after the heart pounding kiss Morgan and I shared a few weeks ago, and many more after that, I had made the decision to send back the latest check and send him back a full refund for all expenses paid. I had never had a client so angry about turning down a job. The snarl in his voice was filled with vengeance. The hairs on my arms actually stool from the tone of his voice. Under normal circumstances, I would have sent him whatever information I obtained on Morgan, but something about this guy had me holding back. He already knew the general location in the city of where Morgan lives and a photo I captured of her while she was sitting outside the bookstore having lunch. I couldn't bring myself to give him any more than that and now, even that seemed to have be too much. I want so badly to tell Morgan who I really am, but I don't want to ruin what is happening between us. Even though I don't know much about her, nothing about her past life, only her San Fran life, she seems so much happier now than the first night I met her. The sadness that was in her eyes that first night is gone, and is now replaced by excitement and maybe even the beginning of love.

Chapter Ten

I couldn't get the excited tone out of my voice. My time with Jack has opened me up to so much happiness and now, to make things hopefully even better, I get to have an official sit down with George Froth from the Art Gallery. George had called me yesterday evening while Jack and I were sitting in my apartment watching movies. George requested a meeting to go over his thoughts about my drawings. By the time the phone conversation ended I found myself standing on top of the couch cushions with Jack holding on to my ankles to keep my balance, I could barely control my excitement.

Sitting in an under–padded chair across from George, I listen to him tell me that my drawings are very good and well–detailed, but they seem to be lacking emotion, my excitement from earlier immediately left my body.

"Now Morgan, Your sketches are superb but I've seen these types of pictures time and time again. If you have anything other than nature sketches, now would be the time to show them. I'm looking to broaden the clientele of this gallery and more tree and pond pictures will not do that".

My head nods in understanding, but at the same time, wondering if the drawings in my shoulder bag would be of any interest to him. These pictures in my bag depict the deepest, darkest times in my past, the secrets never told to anyone other than Louis. These drawing are not something I ever intended on sharing with anyone, especially with a virtual stranger. If George needs to see the emotional side of me, this would be the best way to show him.

Carefully pulling out a sketch pad labeled "Year 17", I slide it across the circular glass table that separates us. I watch George's face while he stares at the sketches, his brows furrow, then raise. He is taking deep staggering breaths that are not helping with the nerves. My hands are holding tight to the sides of my long flowing skirt, I should have worn something more professional looking but I don't own any type of pant suit and I do not have the budget for one. The longer he looks through each piece, the more self-conscious I become. What will he think of me if he realizes it is me in all those drawings.

After what felt like hours, George looks up from the scattered pictures on the table in front of him, with glossed over eyes, he has to clear the lump in his throat before giving me any type of response.

"In all my years of viewing and showcasing art I have never seen both sadness and beauty come through in a sketch before. Morgan, these are truly a sight to see and I thank you for sharing them with me. If you are up for it, I'd like you to choose at least three of these drawings and recreate them onto a large canvas. If you can do it, I will put them up for display during the Fall Art Show."

I look up with some apprehension, not completely believing what was just said. Holding off tears that are threatening to release, I'm finally able to give him the answer I was hoping to.

"Mr. Froth, if you are absolutely certain with this decision, I accept. I accept whole-heartedly".

Clasping his hands together in a small triumphant gesture, George gets up from his seat and walks around the table towards me. He bends down and gives me a little hug causing the held tears to seep from my eyes.

Standing up, I follow George out into the main area of the gallery where we say our goodbyes and plan to touch base in a few weeks to check on my progress. I stand outside on the sidewalk allowing what has just happened, sink in. It has just dawned on me that I have finally permitted someone to have a glimpse into my previous life without them really being aware of the significance of it. I quickly call Avery, then Jack because I'm too excited to wait until I get home to tell them. I don't tell either Jack or Avery which drawings got me the spot in the art show, I'm not ready to answer the questions that will do doubt come when the pictures are complete.

Just before I was about to head out the door to meet Jack for a celebratory drink, I receive a text message from him:

Hey it's me. Will you meet me at my place?

I have a surprise for you

I respond:

Ok, I'll be there soon. You're making me nervous.

Chapter Eleven

Jack meets me outside his apartment building and pulls

me up the stairs to the second floor. He turns me

towards his front door, stepping behind me, he places

both of his hands over my eyes.

"Do you trust me, Morgan?"

The question of trust had never really entered my mind

when it came to Jack, I think I trusted him the moment I

laid my eyes on him that first night.

"Yes, I trust you".

At the same time wanting to say 'More than you'll ever know'.

I'm sensing Jack's apartment is dark and quiet except for the passing vehicles below, I hear nothing but Jack's breath next to my ear. He keeps my eyes covered as we glide down, what must be a hallway. I stretch my arms out and feel my fingertips skimming along the walls on either side of us. We come to a sudden stop in the hallway and I can hear a door creak open in front of me. Jack had removed one of his hands from my face to open the door while keeping the other securely covering my eyes. A clicking sound is made, I can see streams of light coming through the cracks between Jack's fingers. I'm both excited and nervous to see this surprise Jack has set up, I cannot come up with one idea as to what it could be.

"Are you ready to see it?"

"Yes..Yes! I can't remember the last time I got a surprise from someone."

Jack just gives me a little chuckle, obviously amused by my giddiness.

"Alright, Alright. But first I want to tell you how excited I am for you to get this opportunity and I just hope you will share this little part of your life with me".

Jack uncovers my eyes and it takes a moment for my vision to adjust to the brightness in the room. I gasp in awe at what I see before me. The walls are painted the brightest white I have ever seen, lights are hung in each of the four corners casting shadows throughout the small room. Along the back wall, blank canvases of every size are perched up on easels, ready to be transformed into something beautiful. In the center of the room is a simple wooden chest with the absence of a lock. I walk over to it and slowly open the lid. Another more prominent gasp escapes my throat and tears stream down my face at the sight before me. The inside of what can only be described as a treasure chest, is filled with every essential item an artist like me would need. Chalk, charcoal, pencils in every color, oil paints and hog hair brushes. Never in my life have I ever been given such a gift.

"Oh Jack, this is so amazing. Thank you is not even close to the right words to say to you. I can't believe you did this, and for me of all people".

"Morgan, I was glad to do it. You deserve this more than anyone I know. I don't need a thank you, I just like to see you happy".

"I am very happy, Jack. I don't remember the last time I was this happy. Don't think I'm ungrateful, but why me?"

Jack walks over to me, slides his hands to my hips and stares lovingly at me.

"Like I said, I want you to be happy and with this being here, I'll be able to look at you whenever I want to. I want you to be comfortable and enjoy coming here whenever you like. I know it sounds like I had an ulterior motive by doing this, but honestly, your happiness means a lot to me."

In that moment a flash of want surged through my body, a want that I have never experienced in my twenty–one years of living.

Standing up on my tiptoes, I give Jack a chaste kiss on the side of his mouth, lingering a moment to savor the taste. Jack's eyes are dark, full of intensity, there is hunger behind them, hunger for me. He pulls me back towards his body and starts feathering light kisses from my forehead, to my cheek, nose, and down my neck. Jack spends extra time tasting the exposed skin around my collarbone. My body has completely taken over any thoughts of control I had, stripped it away and has replaced it with pure lust. I slide my hands down his arms, feeling the soft hair along them. I slowly start to make my way towards the bottom of his shirt. I want to feel the warmth of his skin pressed against mine, I only want to feel him, see him. My body is on fire, the constant cold inside me has dissipated. I run my short, engine red finger nails along his stomach near the top of his jeans, his muscles tense under my touch. My breath quickens and a small moan escapes from me as Jack's hands travel down my spine and under my shirt to find my bare skin. He continues his sensual assault along my bare back, all the while exploring my mouth with his tongue.

Jack pulls slightly away from me, resting his forehead against mine. He looks up into my eyes,

"Morgan, I need you to tell me what we are doing here"

Trying to keep my breathing under control, I speak through gasped breaths,

"I don't know".

That was as truthful of an answer I could give him. This is the closest I've come to being with a man that wasn't forced upon me. I never imagined I would ever be able to stand a man touching me the way Jack is touching me and I don't want it to end. I want to see what it is like to be touched and caressed by a man that has shown me what it is like to be wanted in such a way that it has my skin tingling with anticipation.

"I've never been with a man like this before."

I feel as if I owe Jack that much of the truth.

"Tell me to stop and I will, Morgan"

His voice is husky as he caresses the exposed skin below my breasts.

Now is the time I should tell him to stop. I opened my mouth to do just that when an embarrassing moan escapes my lips. Why did every touch and kiss feel so much more powerful than I ever could imagine? I should hate this right now, a man taking my control away from me, but I didn't hate it and I realized that I really didn't care and I wanted more, so much more.

Closing my eyes, I took a slow steadying breath, trying to

calm my nerves as my insides burned with heated

passion,

"Don't stop"

Jack stares in to my eyes before initiating the kiss once

again. Our lips met tightly, mouths sweet and slick. As

our mouths devour one another, Jack's hand smoothed

across my cheek and past my ear, before placing it on

the nape of my neck. I couldn't breathe, the sensation of

it all was so intense. It was better than I could have ever

imagined. I tug jack closer, my inexperienced hands

running along his strong body, pulling him close until

there isn't an inch of space between us. I never wanted

anything more that to feel his arms around me and his

lips against mine.

Jack moves his roaming lips down to my neck and softly

sucks on the sensitive spot where my neck meets my

collarbone. I have to bite down on my bottom lip to

suppress a moan as my skin explodes in to flames of heated desire.

Jack's hands never ceasing as they slowly explore every inch of my back, shoulders, and arms. I ran my hands down his shirt, loving the way his crisp cotton shirt feels over his impressive chest and stomach. I think I loved the noises he is making a lot more. It surprised me that I could make him feel this way.

Our hands link together and Jack guides me out of the room he has created for me. He opens the door that leads in to his bedroom. My heart is pounding so hard that I can feel it in my ears. This is really going to happen. Can I actually do this? I am suddenly very nervous at what is about to happen. Jack interrupts my thoughts as he stands beside me, changing gears for a moment to allow me to calm down.

"Sorry about the décor, the bedroom came furnished"

His bedroom is small, much like the size of a walk-in closet owned by a woman with a lot of shoes. I had always thought my place was small, but compared to this, I slept lavishly. A full-size bed sat in the center of the room, pushed up against the wall. Simple navy blue bedding lay upon it. The nightstand next to the bed held only an alarm clock and the remnants of a cup stain. There was no dresser in the room, I don't think one would actually fit, but through the cracked closet door I could see several articles of clothing hanging on white plastic hangers.

As I look around some more, I notice there isn't a single item that could give me an idea of what he likes or who he was before meeting me. No photos or pictures on the walls, no trinkets or family keepsakes either. But then again, I don't have any of that hanging in my room either. I am struck with the notion that I am about to sleep with a man that I really know nothing about, I need to remember how Jack makes me feel whenever we are together and worry about the small stuff later.

I give the room one last glance and look to Jack, silently

thanking him for this calming moment.

"It is nice...small...but who really needs a large room

anyway"

Jack laughs almost too loud, nervous have collided with

him as well.

"You are being too kind, but it works for now."

I enter further in to the room with Jack trailing. As I

reach the edge of the bed Jack comes up behind me

quickly and wraps his arms around my waist. I was not

prepared for his playful abruptness, I stumble forwards

and fall on to the bed. Memories flash before my eyes, I

tense up immediately at the thought of being forced to

my stomach on the bed. I scramble to my feet in an

alarm, unable to control the panicked feeling that has

washed over me. Jack senses my reaction. He takes a

step back and turns me around to face him. Concern is

the only way to describe the way Jack is looking at me.

"Morgan, look at me. Is everything okay? We can stop if that's what you want."

I look in to his beautiful eyes and I know right then that everything will be just fine. Jack would never do anything to purposely hurt me. He knows nothing of my past, so how was he supposed to know that being even the slightest bit rough would put me into a panic.

"No no..I want this, but can you promise me one thing?"

"Anything"

"Promise me you won't force me on to my stomach"

Jack's face went strangely blank, not sure what to think of a request of that nature.

"I'm sorry, I should have never said that, just forget about it."

I was starting to get flustered, and I'm sure I was ruining the moment. Covering my face with my hands to hid my embarrassment, Jack must think I'm some naïve little girl, in a way I am naïve, but not for the lack of wanting.

Feeling a smooth caress to my hands, Jack grabs ahold of them and brings them slowly to his lips. He kisses the tips of my fingers softly and stares into the depth of my soul, casting all the reassurance and devotion that I need to ease the tension.

"Morgan, I need you to listen to me...I will never do anything to you that you do not want done. We can take this slow and see where it goes...okay?"

I release a hand from his grasp and run it along his strong cheek bone, I am in awe of this man. How could I get so lucky to have someone like this standing in front of me?

I step forward, closing the gap between us. I raise up on my tiptoes, stopping before my lips touch his.

"Okay...but, one more thing..."

"Anything you need."

"I need you to teach me..."

"Now, that... is something I can do."

When I grab at the hem of my tank top to pull it up, my hands are gently brushed away. Jack kisses me again as he slowly pulls my shirt up, taking his time to run the back of his knuckles over my stomach then up along my breasts. I let out a small moan as his knuckles glide over my erect nipples, causing a painful erotic sensation to flow through me. Jack breaks the kiss only long enough to finish pulling my top off then his mouth was back on mine. I can feel his massive erection press against my waist, he feels so good against me, but I need him to be much closer.

I made a quick effort at removing Jack's shirt, finally getting the opportunity to trace my fingers along his tattoos, taking my time tracing his sister's initials above his heart. I couldn't stop there, I needed to see him in all his glory. My hands were shaking at I worked on unbuttoning his jeans. Jacks hands replaced my and he swiftly pulled his jeans and boxer-briefs down in succession.. I just simply stood there staring at him, dumbfounded.

Grinning, Jack walks over to me and pulls me in to his arms. His lips meet mine and I couldn't help but sigh. He was an amazing kisser, he certainly knew what he was doing. I just hoped I was giving him the same satisfaction.

I became quite daring, which surprised me. I sat down on to the bed, stripping out of my shorts and panties. Once undressed, I started crawling backwards onto it. The bed dipped as Jack followed me. As soon as my back is rested against the headboard, jack leans forward to take my mouth in a heated kiss, his hands once again roaming my body.

He trailed his fingers up and between my breasts and continued to move his hand up until he was cupping my face, lovingly stoking my jawline. His mouth trailed kisses down to the opposite side of my neck and his hand moved back down and cups one of my breasts in his warm hand. I bit back a small cry and I have to close my eyes from the feeling of his touch. I wrap my arms around his shoulder, needed to added support while

Jacks continues his exploration. I have never in my life felt this wanted, all his movements are unrushed, taking his time learning my body.

I take a deep breath to steady my nerves, the heat between my legs is begging to be released. I can't think past how good Jack is making me feel, I need him and nothing else seemed to matter but this moment.

Jack brings himself up and his erection brushes against my too sensitive skin. I have to shift my legs, the growing need inside me was almost too much to bare. I am unable to wait another minute, I reach down and grasp onto his length guiding it between my legs, his large tip coming to a halt at my entry,

"Are you sure?"

Jack pulls his lips from mine and stares intently.

"Yes, I'm definitely sure."

My words come out in a harsh whisper, I need him, now. Taking his erection back into my hand, I slowing start to nudge it inside me, along my folds until the tip is slowing expanding my walls.

"Wait..wait a second."

Breathing heaving, Jack pulls away from me. For a short second I thought I had done something wrong, that he wasn't enjoying himself as much as I was. It wasn't until he reached into his nightstand that I understand what was happening. How could I forget something so simple as protection, this is something that was drilled into our heads at freshman in high school. This just shows how inexperienced I really am.

Watching Jack rolls the condom along his length scared me for a moment, the realization that this was going to happen hit me like a ton of bricks. But, if I'm going to do this, I'm glad it's with someone who has worked to gain my trust and companionship.

Getting back in to position, Jack rests himself back in between my thighs. An unexpected moan escapes my lips as Jack gently slides into me, filling me only halfway before pulling back out. I hang on to him tight, almost begging him to return before he thrusts back into me, this time completely filling me. I don't know whether to cry out in pleasure or pain, I have never felt pleasure like this, only pain. But with just two thrusts, I never want this feeling to stop.

Jack brings his hands to my face, cupping both cheeks and kisses me hard and long, our tongues dancing with one another. I begin to roll my hip in sync with his movements, a steady, electrifying rhythm. Jack's answering moans was all the encouragement I needed to know that I was doing just fine. We pick up the pace, Jack trusting hard, taking me further and deeper. My mind is spinning and my insides are over heating with a building sensation of my approaching climax.

I can feel Jack growing inside me. I don't know how much longer I can hang on, the warmth inside me was getting to be too much. He felt so good, too good. A loud growl comes from deep within Jacks throat, he trusts harder and harder. I dig my nails into his back, trying so hard to hang on. I can't..

A rush of pleasure hits me with so much force that my toes curl to no end, my whole body is shaking as I climax. It's a never-ending, amazing feeling running through my body. The perfect end to this experience is the moment Jack gave one last hard thrust into me before crying out my name in pure satisfaction.

For several minutes after, Jack and I just lay still, holding each other tight, it was another perfect moment. I felt so relaxed and cherished and...happy. My head rests on his chest, finger splayed across him making little circles along his stomach. Jack runs his soft lips through my tangled hair. Neither one wanting to move, for if we do the moment will be over with. I could lay here in his arms forever and be happy and content. A long, stifling yawn flows out of my mouth and a rumbling in Jacks chests brings on a fit of giggles.

"Did I wear you out?"

"You most certainly did, Mr. Sloan."

"Just close your eyes, I'll just hang back and watch you sleep."

I snuggle into the side of his body more, fitting perfectly, like I was made to lay my body against his.

"Are you sure you're okay will me sleeping here?"

Jack runs his hand down my arm until he reaches my hand. He brings it up to his lips placing a soft kiss inside the palm of my hand.

"I wouldn't want it any other way. Now, get some sleep. I'll be right here when you wake up."

Chapter Twelve

Stretching my legs out, I can feel the soreness throughout my body, a soreness I would gladly take just to do that over and over again. Never have I dreamt that it could feel so amazing. It felt like Jack was so in tune with what I was feeling and sensing my nervousness. He was so kind and patient with me, never rushing a single moment. I look over and steal a glance at the beautiful creature, watching the steady rise and fall of his chest. I want to run my fingers through the small patch of hair that runs along the top of his boxer briefs to his belly button, feel what's under those briefs that has me desiring for more. I hold off on that urge for now and quietly slip out of bed, wrapping the dark blue cotton sheet around my naked body. I don't want to wake him just yet. I make my way to the bathroom to clean myself up. Standing in front of the mirror, it is the first time I can look at myself with a genuine smile on my face. In this moment, I have made a heart pounding discovery...I'm falling in love with Jack Sloan. I feel as if I'm floating on a cloud high in the sky where no one can bring me down.

I finish up in the bathroom and getting dressed, I decide to take a peek around Jack's apartment since this was the first time coming here. Jack lives in a small two bedroom apartment, much like mine and Avery's except his second room is more for storage. The apartment is in Chinatown. If only I knew Jack last winter, we could have experienced Chinatown's Community Street fair together, or just viewed it all right from his window. Even though it is early morning, I can already smell the makings of gourmet foods from the Chinese culture. I can imagine the taste of the beef dumplings exploding my taste buds.

I look around the main area of the apartment, there is a small metal futon off in the corner with a floor lamp next to it. The walls are bare, no pictures hanging to give me some idea as to where he has come from, but then again we did strike a deal of no questions. With Jack being a photographer, you would think he would have at least a few of his pictures somewhere, I have yet to see any. There are no curtains hung, the light streams through the exposed window. I walk over to it and look down at the busy street below. So many people rushing here and there, not taking the time to stop and enjoy all the pleasures around them.

Stepping away from the window, I continue my tour of his place. The kitchen is no bigger than something you would see in a hotel room. A dorm size fridge is set up on the floor with a hot plate for cooking sitting on top. The doors on the cupboards are warped from age and have been stripped of their varnish. Opening one cupboard, I can instantly tell he doesn't get much company. Two plates, a bowl, and one chipped coffee cup rests on a layer of dust, which is not much for dinnerware even for oneself. Walking away from the nonexistent kitchen, I find myself kneeling down next to a small tan filing cabinet near the front door. I don't care to snoop, but there is something about this cabinet that has compelled me to take a look inside.

The top two drawers are filled with nothing but legal documents pertaining to his lease agreement, bank and tax statements. The third drawer sticks a little when I open it, making a grinding noise like a car door sounds when the hinges need to be greased. Pulling open the drawer the rest of the way, I find several alphabetical files. Grabbing the first one, I slide it out and open it up. The manila folder is filled with personal information on a particular man named Michael Franklin Alders. Photographs of this man have been shot from a distance, most pictures are of Mr. Alders and several beautiful women. I put the file back in order and place it back into the file cabinet, I move on to the next one. Once again, I find the same things in the other folders. I sit back wondering why Jack would have this kind of information and photos of all these people. It just doesn't make any sense for a photographer to have this. The only thing that I can think of is that Jack must be hiding something of his own. With everything back in place, I shut the drawer and stand back up off the floor. As I'm walking away from the cabinet something catches my eye. A photograph is wedged between the file cabinet and a small personal shredder that is set on top of a black garbage can. I slide the garbage can over, being careful not to knock off the shredder. Sliding it away just enough to easily grab the photo. Picking it up and turning it over, all the air immediately leaves my lungs. I feel as if the wind has been knocked out of me after a hard punch in the gut. I can hardly move, I slowly drag my feet along the hard wood surface of the floor and collapse onto the futon. "Why does Jack have this picture? How did he get this picture?" I never saw the picture, I refused to look at it, but I remember that day very well. It was a reminder that my life before now was

nothing but agony and misery.

Chapter Thirteen

My father was in one of his moods where you didn't dare cross him and if you did, you wouldn't be able to go to school for the next several days or until the marks faded. I was fifteen in this picture. My father decided it was a great day for a family photo, except I was the only person that was going to be in the photo. He wanted a picture to remind me of the disappointing daughter I had become.

My father made me put on the only dress I had, which hadn't fit me since I was thirteen. The dress had a white lace top, yellow satin skirt with white daisies embroidered on it. At thirteen, this dress was the prettiest of all the other dresses at the Easter Sunday service. That was what my father had told me throughout that blessed day. But as a fifteen year old, being told to wear that dress and doing so, I was a sinner and a whore. My father's words ring loud in my ears, "You will be greatly punished for your indecent behavior! You are nothing but a little whore, and you will be treated as a whore!"

My father was not always an evil man, as a young child he was the one person that could always solve all my problems. We lived a simple life in Maine in a beautiful two story colonial style home. The large bay windows allowed the morning sunrise to heat up the cool ceramic tiles in the kitchen. A porch swing on the front deck was put there for dad and I to talk while drinking hot cocoa with tiny marshmallows as the sun went down in the evenings. My father was the lead engineer for power companies across the Northern East Coast. Although his work could keep him away for long hours, he always made it home to tuck me into bed. Our life consisted of beach days on the weekends, picnics in the park with the ducks, Daddy/Emma slumber parties with scary movies and stove popped popcorn. The only thing that was missing from our lives was my mother. I had never met her, my father said she left us shortly after I was born. I always avoided asking questions about her because it seemed to upset him. All I know is her name; Elizabeth Reece.

Life was grand in the Reece household. Just my dad and myself.

Things started to become different just after I became an official teenager, the milestone I wish I would have never reached.

At the time, the longer hugs and bigger kisses, the soft caressing to the hair just seemed embarrassing and slightly uncomfortable, nothing more. He would get angrier much easier if I pulled away too quick, but I just thought that he didn't think I loved him enough, so I made sure to never pull away from his embrace.

A child doesn't notice changes in things that an adult normally would. Thinking back, now as an adult, I notice. I was fourteen when my father stole my innocence.

My joy filled life ended when Charlie Johnson came into my world. It's not every day a gorgeous, popular sophomore shows an interest in a younger girl, but when he set his sights on me, the tall skinny, underdeveloped freshman, I was over and beyond the moon. Our courtship was strictly within the school grounds so my father had no idea I was dating, I enjoyed this little secret. The thought of it being a big deal to him, never crossed my mind, I never saw any point in mentioning it to him. I was wrong, so very wrong.

Charlie and I shared what young teenagers considered passionate kisses, which meant there was a lot of spit and way too much tongue involved. We held hands while walking me to my classes and passed love notes in the hallways of the school. We had quite the teenage romance going.

The homecoming dance was right around the corner and Charlie didn't hesitate asking me to be his date, nor did I hesitate in saying yes.

I had made the decision to lie to my father, something I wasn't in the habit of doing. I was worried he would tell me I was too young to date or that Charlie was too old for me. Thinking I was being smart, I came to the conclusion of telling my father that I was going to the homecoming football game and then over to my friend, Stephanie's for a horror movie marathon. It wasn't hard to convince my dad that's what I was doing since, to his knowledge, I never lied before.

The night of homecoming, I packed my backpack with a scoop neck, deep purple dress Stephanie let me borrow and a pair of the highest silver high heeled shoes I could find at the exchange store downtown. With my makeup and clothes for the dance packed away in my bag, I slid up my bedroom window and popped out the screen, resting it against the wall. As gently as I could, I dropped my backpack down to the ground from the second floor. Throwing the teams jersey over my white cotton tee and jeans, I left my room in search of my converse sneakers. Putting on my shoes at the kitchen table next to my dad, I watch as he takes a long swallow of his second or third beer, he looks at me, almost glaring when he tells me to be home no later than eleven o'clock. By the look on his face, I thought for sure he had found out the real plan for tonight.

With a timid, innocent smile, I stood from the table and made my way out the door. I quietly crept around the side of the house to get my backpack. Once the bag was in my hands, I took off in a dead sprint into the woods behind our house. I ran as fast as I could until I knew I was far enough away to come out onto the road. There was no way I was going to let this night with Charlie be ruined by anything or anyone, not even my dad.

The dance was in full swing when Charlie and I walked in. Hand in hand, Charlie pulled me out on to the dance floor. I felt like a princess with the flower on my wrist that Charlie had bought for me and the twinkling lights around us. We danced and laughed, and smiled for hours, I was the happiest girl alive.

With my curfew fast approaching, Charlie offered to walk me home. We walked together in a comfortable silence until my house was coming in to view. Charlie took my hand and pulled me into the trees along a walking path at the edge of our property line. Leaning me against the nearby tree, Charlie kissed me hard while running the palm of his hand on my breast outside my dress. After a few minutes of this, Charlie gave me one last goodbye kiss and walked away along the trail. Still hiding in the trees I unzipped my backpack and pulled out my jeans and jersey to change back in to. Changing against a tree as giddy as I was, became a difficult task, but after several trips and mumbling remarks, I finally managed to look presentable to go home. A voice spoke from somewhere close as I was shoving my dress and shoes back into my bag.

"Did you enjoy yourself out here with that boy, Emma?"

I look all around me trying to find the source of the voice, that can only be my father. I finally see the outline of a man in between a tree and a lilac bush. Even though I can't see his face, the tone of his voice tells me he is very angry. I've never really been scared of my father, until this moment.

"I asked you a question Emma. Did you enjoy yourself?!"

Not know what the right answer to the question is, I tell him the truth, no use in lying to him twice in one night.

"Yes I did, Dad. Charlie is a very nice boy and we really like each other".

This was the moment my father became the devil incarnate, I should have lied again.

My father charges towards me with anger filled eyes, grabbing me by my curled hair and drags me towards the back door. He was mumbling things under his breath that I had never heard him say before, 'slut...whore...slut.. whore..' again and again. Tuning out his words wasn't hard with the pain in my scalp being so intense.

My father continued pulling me by a handful of hair through the house and up the stairs. He opened my bedroom door and threw me to the ground with so much force my knees stung from the fall.

"STAND UP AND FACE ME, EMMA!"

I stand up quickly, but keep my head down staring at my feet.

"I'm sorry for lying to you, I really wanted to go and I thought you would say no, so I lied. I promise it will never happen again".

"Did you enjoy behaving like a little whore tonight?"

The air in my lungs leaves in a whoosh at his words, I looked up and stare at a man that is clearly not acting like my father.

"How can you say such a thing, Dad?! Just because I

kissed Charlie, it doesn't make me a bad person!"

SMACK

My ears are ringing from the blow to the side of my face. That was the last time I ever talked back to my father, or really spoke to him for that matter.

I have never been hit before, not even a spanking as a young child, and certainly not a stinging slap across the face. After these moments, he was no longer the man that was my hero, my protector. He became the monster not under, but in my bed.

"Turn around and take off your clothes. If you want to act like a whore than you are going to be punished like a whore".

Hesitating too long brought another round of slaps, too hard and fast for me to react.

Turning away from my father, I removed my shirt and pants. I stood there in only my bra and panties, shaking from both the coolness in my room and the sobs of terror escaping me.

"STOP CRYING! Whores don't cry. They don't get the privilege of any emotions!"

I close my eyes and listen to the sounds around me. I can hear the television on downstairs, the grandfather clock in the dining room making a soft ticking sound and then I hear the unfastening of a metal belt buckle, my father's belt. Oh please no, please no. I'm unable to control my whimpers as my father brings the belt down on me.

SNAP!

I scream

SNAP! SNAP!

I scream even harder. Never have I experienced such pain, I could already feel the welts forming on my back. My father then pushes me down onto the bed, pinning me to the mattress with his strong, angry hands. I can smell the strong stench of alcohol on his breath, he leans down rubbing his mustache along my cheek and whispers bitterly into my ear,

"You want to act like a whore, then I will treat you like

one"

He lifts his body further onto the bed, hovering over

me,spining my body over so my stomach is flat against

the bed. I can hear him digging into his pocket, I glance

to the side and watch him pull out his black serrated

switch blade that he keeps on him at all times. I start to

squirm under his body but that only seems to agitate

him more. He lifts his knee and pushes it into my back,

halting all efforts to get free from him. I can feel the

blade of the knife as he runs it along my outer thigh and

reaching my hip bone. My father grips onto the elastic

band, slices it in half causing my panties to sage loose

around me.

I lay there completely exposed except for my bra. I try

not to think about what is going to happen next but

hearing the gruff moans from my father behind me

makes me think of every possible scenario, wishing

deeply for the pain of the belt to come back, instead of

what is about to happen. He sits with one knee on my back, the other on the side of my body while he vigorously rubs himself. Squeezing my eyes shut as my father starts to slowly shift his weight lower, caressing his penis along my bare behind until he comes to a stop at the entrance of my most private and sacred spot. I immediately tense up more, tugging and pulling on whatever I can reach, needing to get out from under him.

"STAY STILL you little slut! You know you like it! All whores like it!"

"Daddy, Please! Stop..Stop..PLEASE!"

Hot searing pain spreads between my legs as my father shoves his furious force into me. The more I beg and plead for him to stop, the harder he pushes in to me.

Time stands still, the world around me no longer exists. I am dead. My soul has been ripped from my body, I am empty. I don't know how long this went on for but he finally stopped. He pulled out and continued stoking himself behind me. Wet, warm liquid hit the top of my tailbone just as my father released a gratifying moan. No regard for what he has done to me, he stands up, puts his pants on, leaving them unbuttoned as a fair warning.

"Clean this mess up, you dirty whore!"

I lay there not moving, scared to move, scared he will come back. I can feel the dampness on my sheets and realize the moisture is not from my tears or his sweat, it is blood. My inner thighs and pale pink sheets are covered in blood, my blood.

My life became a series of lashings with the belt and daily beatings with his fists. My father was smart though, he made sure to never hit me hard enough to leave a lasting mark, but hard enough to make me keep quiet about what went on behind closed doors.

The day this picture was taken, was the day my father saw me smiling at a boy from class while we were shopping at the grocery store. When we got home, I was told to change into that too small Easter dress and be reminded of what happens to whores who try corrupting the minds of young men. He brought me outside to stand in front of the lilac bushes where this all started and smile for a picture. My father than walked me back inside, took me upstairs, followed me in to my bedroom, locking the door securely behind him. This day was the second time I was raped by my father.

I learned after that second time,as long as I never showed any emotion I could get away with just the beatings. I walked the streets and halls at school like I was already dead, never speaking to anyone unless it was absolutely necessary. I never cried or laughed, and most certainly never smiled at another person for the next three years.

Chapter Fourteen

Jack...

Reaching out in search of her warm body, needing to feel her soft, pale skin at my fingertips again, I come up empty. Looking over, Morgan is not there. I know last night wasn't a dream because I can still smell the scent of her ginger perfume on my pillow. Last night had been amazing, the best night with a woman I've ever had. Our connection sparked something deep inside me. I think I may be falling in love with this woman. I climb out of bed quickly, feeling the need to find her just to be near her again. Pulling on a pair of sweatpants, I walk into the living room, but stop. Morgan is sitting on the edge of the futon with her head down, holding a picture in her hands. She looks deep in thought and on the verge of tears. I start to make my way towards her when she raises one of her hands, prompting me to stop.

"Stop. Do not come any closer to me".

"Morgan. What's going on? You're freaking me out here. Did I hurt you last night? Oh God, I'm so sorry if I did."

I raise my hand to her, wanting so badly to comfort her, but she just shakes her head in a silent plea to stay put where I stand.

She finally looks at me, there is so much pain and hurt in her eyes.

"Why do you have this picture?"

Morgan flips over the photo she is holding, allowing me to see which one she is talking about.

"Morgan, I can explain."

"Who the hell are you? And why do you have this picture?!"

"You already know who I am, Jack Sloan."

"Quit lying to me! Why would a photographer have a picture of me when I was fifteen?!"

I feel completely defeated, caught in the act by the women I never wanted to hurt.

"I am Jack, you know me. I've wanted to tell you the truth since the first time I kissed you. I just didn't want to ruin what we have."

"Answer me now! Why?!"

"I have your picture because I was hired to find you. Actually, I was hired to find Emma Reece."

Like a hissing, venomous snake Morgan starts yelling at me, rage filling her voice.

"Don't you ever call me that! My name is Morgan James, Emma died a long time ago".

"Morgan, I'm sorry. I swear to you that I turned away the job once I started to get to know you, and after last night I think I may be falling in love with you."

"Don't you dare say that, and don't you dare talk to me about last night! I trusted you! Do you have any idea how hard that was for me to do?!"

"Please believe me, I never meant to hurt you".

"Too late. So, us bumping into each other at the bar was just you doing your job?"

"That was a coincidence! Honest! After showing that picture around the area, several people thought they remembered seeing you at the Cove. I started hanging out in there from time to time to see if you'd show. Having you bump in to me was the best thing that has ever happened, and after I kissed you that first time I knew I couldn't continue with the job."

"Who hired you? Was it the cops?!"

"No...Wait, What?"

"Who hired you, then?!"

"A guy named Stanley Reece. He said he was your father".

"No! You're lying! No No!"

"I'm not lying! He said you ran away and he really wanted to find you and that picture was the most recent one he could find".

"No. That's not possible, it can't be".

I wasn't sure if Morgan was telling me this or reassuring herself that it wasn't her father. She was up on her feet now, pacing the floor. The picture lay crumpled in a ball on the ground.

Speaking softly to her,

"Morgan, why isn't it possible? He seemed determined to find you."

Morgan stops her pacing and gives a vacant look towards the window, she whispers softly, almost to herself.

"Because I killed him three years ago when he tried to rape me again".

Silence.

The room was dead silent except for the outside noise.

Too stunned with Morgan's revelation, I don't hear the front door click shut.

Chapter Fifteen

I run out of the apartment and straight into a group of people. It feels as if every one of them is reaching and grabbing for me. Like they're all on his side, working for him. The walls around my vision are closing in and I'm finding it difficult to catch my breath.

I saw his lifeless body covered in the blood I shed, how could he be alive? I keep running through the crowd of people, running until my legs are burning like the fire that should have burned him. I can feel all eyes on me, being watched by him. Watched by the man I was sure died three years ago.

I finally stop running when I reach the pier along the water, my lungs begging for air to pass through them. I sit down on a green painted bench at the far end of the pier. It's like I am back in that nightmare all over again, I can feel my father's hands on my body and his belt thrashing against my back. Even though I know it is just in my subconscious, I still wince from the reminder of the pain. I can't help but look all around me, feeling his eyes on me, waiting for me to make a mistake and cry for the evil that he is, that evil that took away the rest of my childhood. I want to cry for the man that will now be lost to me because he knows the worst parts of me, my scars have been exposed to him. How could any man love me for allowing this to go on for as long as it did?

Finally arising from my trance, I realize dusk is approaching. My bare feet ache from running here without shoes and I am starting to get chilled in my shorts and Jack's long t-shirt. Even in mid–August, the breeze off the water makes the air seem much colder. I walk only a little way until I reach a cable car that will take me back up town towards our apartment. I just need to get home, change my clothes, and start figuring out my next move. I'm not about to stick around and find out what was waiting for me.

"Jack called. Are you okay?"

I should have known he would call her when I didn't answer my phone.

"No, actually. I am not okay and if what Jack says is true, I have to get out of here or I will never be okay".

"But Jack said he turned down the job, so there is no reason to run. We can figure things out together. Okay?"

"Avery, I don't think you understand how serious this is. I can't just sit back and hope it isn't true. If he is still alive then he will be looking for me, and won't stop until he either kills me or takes me back!"

Racing to my room, ignoring Avery's efforts to calm me down, but all I can't think about is getting far away from this place. Even if my father doesn't know exactly where I am, he will find a way. If Jack found me by flashing a picture, it won't be difficulty for my father to find me either. Clothes are being thrown over my shoulder in a frantic attempt to pack whatever I can fit in a small bag, hangers that held them are ricocheting off every surface of the room.

Oblivious to what's going on around me, Avery grabbed ahold of my shoulders, adding pressure while trying to shake some sense into me.

"Morgan! Morgan, stay with me! Don't you dare space out on me now. If we are going to stick this out together, I need you to tell me what is going on and who the hell are you so scared of?!"

Defeated, I collapse to the ground in a hysterical fit. Through blurred eyes, I look to Avery, who is pleading with me to let her in, let her help me.

"I'm scared of my father. I'm so scared, Avery. It's no

use. No matter where I go, he will find me."

Chapter Sixteen

Jack...

Two weeks went by and Morgan has yet to return any of my messages. My dad keeps telling me to give her time to figure things out, trust has been broken and that isn't something that can be earned back in couple weeks. I should have never lied to her, I told myself I would eventually tell her the truth, but the time never seemed right. Thankfully, Avery agreed to meet me for coffee to help me understand what is going on with Morgan and how things went so wrong for her.

Avery doesn't even have a chance to sit down with her iced mocha before I start in.

"How is she?"

"Her nightmares are back..."

Avery looks down at her hands that are wrapped tightly around her drink. Her eyes begin to moisten when she looks back up to me.

"She's scared, Jack. She doesn't want to believe that her Father is actually alive, but deep down I think she knows it's true. I have never seen her so terrified before. Every time she steps out of the apartment building she constantly looks around as if someone is going to jump out at her. She has all the windows shut and locked and she even started sleeping with a deadbolt on her bedroom door...when she does eventually sleep. Aside from not sleeping, she isn't eating much either. I pretty much have to force feed her like a child. I just don't know how to make things easier for her. "

Running my hands across the stubble on my chin, I close my eyes and ask Avery the question that I'm not sure I am prepared to hear, but I need to know what happened to her so I can find a way to help her.

"Did she tell you anything about what happened with him?"

"After that morning with you, she came home so scared that she was ready to pack a bag and run off again. I convinced her to stay and tell me what has happened to her".

Setting down my black coffee after taking a sip, I try to mentally prepare myself for what's to be said.

"Did she really try to kill him?"

"Yes. Until two weeks ago, she thought she succeeded".

Not sure if I actually wanted to hear the details, but needing to know, I had to ask what went on in that home.

"Avery, what happened?"

Folding her hands around her coffee cup, Avery begins telling the story of the day Morgan thought she had killed her Father.

"She said she had it all planned out to leave town. It was a week after her graduation and her father was supposed to be gone for a couple days checking on a new jobsite. She had already cleared out her bank account and had a bag packed underneath her bed. Morgan had made it down only three stairs when her father appeared at the bottom landing. She didn't know how he had found out her plan, but he knew. She said she could tell by the hard, straight line of his mouth and the glare of his eyes. He stalked up the stairs after her and she took off running to her room and hid in the back of the closet. Stan had found her quickly and drug her out by her feet and started pulling her towards the bed, all the while screaming that she was nothing but an ungrateful child and she was never leaving that house. Morgan wasn't about to let him touch her again so she kicked at him and kicked some more until he lost his grip on her ankles. She scrambled to her feet, but her dad was too fast and caught up to her. He held her tight around the chest at the top of the stairs trying to drag her back to the room. Morgan threw her head back as hard as she could and hit him right in the nose. Her dad's arms loosened around her as he stumbled backwards. Morgan watched as her dad lost his balance on the top step and sailed through the air, falling hard in a heap at the bottom of the staircase. She slowly approached his mangled body, legs and arms sprawled out every which way, blood coming from his ears and nose. She couldn't see his chest rise, but couldn't herself to get a closer look. Morgan ran back into her room, grabbed her backpack and took off through the back door. Unsure of what to do, she search around in the small storage shed, finding full gas cans. Not wanting any trace or memory of the house or the man lying dead inside, Morgan gripped cans tightly in her hands towards the back door. Her father's body still lying in the same spot at the stairs. She started in the kitchen and worked her way to the living-room, splattering the gas along the floor until she reached the back door again. She pulled out a book of matches from her pocket, struck the match, and dropped it onto the puddle of gas just inside the door. Morgan hid in the woods and watched the house fill with flames and smoke, watched as the man who ruined her childhood, burned within the walls of a home that had taken away any sense of comfort and warmth. Even with the madness of it all, Morgan said she felt a sense of peace after what she had done, and never regret."

More silence.

How does someone live with themselves with they find out they may have helped a monster hunt down the woman they love.

The was no more room for words, nothing could be said to make this right for anyone.

With tears falling down her cheek, Avery rose from her seat, giving me a silent goodbye.

"Avery?"

"Yeah, Jack?"

"Can you please tell Morgan that I love her, and I'll be here for her whenever she is ready."

"Okay"

Avery turned away from me and walked out the door.

Incapable of believing the horrible things that Morgan had went through, It's ripping me up inside. I want to go to Maine and find her father and kill him myself for what he did to her. What sick bastard could do that to someone, let alone his own child? I need to find a way to get Morgan to talk to me, show her I will always be there to love and protect her. I will never let anyone hurt her like that again.

Even after my sister's passing, I have never been this angry at someone, I can barely control the rage boiling through me. Closing my fist, I slam it into the wall as hard as I can. A cloud of drywall dust clouds around the hole my fist created. Drops of blood fall to the floor as I remove my fist from the wall. Walking to the sink to rinse off my injured hand, there is a knock on the door. A white envelope is slipped under the crack in the door and stops at my feet. I pick up the envelope and open the door, but no one is there. Stepping back in to the apartment, I close the door and examine the front. There is no return address, with my name underlined in the center of it. I turn it over and rip it open along the licked seal. Oh god. My heart feels like it's pounding out of my chest and the rage fills within me once again as I stare at the picture before me. I'm holding the same picture of

Morgan sitting outside Bracken Bookstore, that I sent to him before quitting the search. Turning over the photo, gasping as I read what has been written on the back,

"THANKS FOR YOUR HELP. PLAYTIME IS OVER."

Dropping the picture to the ground, I throw open my front door, it to crash against the wall putting another fresh hole in it. I don't bother locking the door as I race down the stairs and out the main doors. The only thing that is going through my mind is getting to Morgan and making sure she is safe. I pull out my phone and dial her number, it goes straight to voicemail. Shit! I quickly scroll through my contacts and find Avery's name, pressing send,

"Hello?"

"Avery! Oh thank god! Are you with Morgan?"

"No, I'm just finishing up on some shopping. Why, What's up? You sound out of breath."

"I think her dad is here! Someone slid a photo of her

under my door and there was a message on the back of it. Oh god, Avery. I can't get through to her on her phone!"

"Oh no! I'm on my way home. I'll try her cell and you keep trying too!"

"Okay. I'm on my way there also. Avery, we have to get her out of there, get her as far away from here as possible."

"I Know."

Chapter Seventeen

I know I should answer my phone, it's been a couple weeks since I heard his voice and I miss him, but I'm not sure if I am ready to face Jack yet. I'm so ashamed with myself for ever letting this happen to me, pissed off that he lied to me, scared, and tired of running. Mostly, I don't want to see the pity that will be in his eyes. How can someone love you, but pity you at the same time? Jack is the one person that makes me feel beautiful, not a disgusting girl my father made me believe I always was. Jack has stolen my heart and I'm almost certain that I don't want him to give it back.

My phone continues to ring again and again. Walking over to the nightstand where I had set it down, I look at the screen and see it is Avery calling me. Jack must have called her to try and convince me to talk to him. I pick up my phone to answer it just as a knock sounds at the door, apparently Jack couldn't take a hint and just came over instead. Hitting the answer button on my cell and cutting off Avery's loud rant on the other end of the line,

"Yeah, yeah Avery. I know I need to talk to Jack. I'm just worried he isn't going to look at me like he did before he found out about what happened to me. I am going to talk to him now, I'm sure it's him banging on our door right now. I'll let you know how it went later".

I could hear Avery yelling for me to wait when I hit the end button on the cell phone.

Opening the door, not bothering to look through the peephole, I take a sharp intake of breath as I see who is standing before me.

"Oh god..."comes out barely above a whisper.

"Hello, My dear Emma. Did you miss me?"

Trying hard to shut the door, but the steel toes of his

boots is blocking it from shutting all the way. I put all my 120 pounds of weight into securing the door but it's no use, he's too strong. My father easily pushes against it, knocking me back into the apartment,

"What are you doing here? GET OUT!"

"Now, now, Emma. Is that anyway to speak to your father? I thought I raised you better."

"My name is NOT Emma!"

"Oh, yes of course, so I've heard...Morgan."

My breathing is becoming erratic at just the sight of this horrible man. This man that is supposed to be dead...How can this be? I saw his lifeless body, I struck a match...this can't be real. Wake up, Morgan...please wake from this nightmare.

"How?...How are you..."

"How do I know your name, Morgan James? Or how am I not dead?"

The distain in his voice has me backing away from his

slow, slithering pursuit, but he continues to move step by little step closer.

"I do have to say, trying to burn the house with me still inside was a nice touch, but not nice enough".

This time, I don't back down from him, I glare right back at the monster.

"Obviously not."

My father laughs in my face, still knowing that I'm not as tough as I'm trying to act, he knows I'm still the scared little girl he ruined.

"Did you think I would just let you get away with what you tried doing to me, or that I would even let you get away from me?!"

"What I did to you!? What about what you did to me? You are one sick bastard, you know that?!"

"Someone had to teach you a lesson, you ungrateful whore!"

After years of abuse and torment, I can no longer

contain my anger, I let myself snap. Lunging at him, my fists clenched and swinging like a mad woman, igniting years for rage that can't be extinguished. Instant pain shoots through my right hand as my fist connects with his chin, I scream out in agony. Letting my guard down in that brief moment, my father holds tight and tackles me hard to the ground.

"You stupid, STUPID BITCH!"

I try to get back up on my feet, ignoring the searing pain in my hand, but my father doesn't let me get far. I start to scream out hoping someone can hear me,

"HELP! Please somebody, Help me!"

My father clamps a hand over my mouth, halting any more efforts of me calling out. He pins me on my back, pushing my head down on to the hardwood floors beneath me. He raises a hand and smacks me on the left side of my head with so much force, my ears ring from the blow.

"You will keep your mouth shut! This will only be worse

on you if you try and pull another stunt like that."

I start to wonder if it is even worth it to fight him off, I've never been able to win against him before. What makes this time any different? Lying here underneath my father's heavy weight, knowing imminent death is upon me, I think of the people who have changed my life, allowed me to expose my scars and still chose to see me. Giving myself a moment, I see Jack, Avery, and even Cole. Avery has shown me what it's like to have a sister and a best friend. Cole has been a constant sight of happiness, you can't help but smile when you are around him. And Jack...oh Jack. Even with his lie looming over us, I can honestly say I have finally felt what real love is supposed to feel like. It hit me like a wave, my love for Jack. Even though it has only been a few months of knowing him, it feels like forever. I regret not telling him this, but I refuse to give myself over to my father without Jack knowing he has my heart.

Refusing to let this go on any longer, I reach my good

hand up and grab ahold of my father's hair, gripping it tightly until he is forced to remove his hand from my mouth, I don't let go as I continue to scream again.

"HEELLLLPPP! HELLLLPPP SOMEONE!..."

My father still has a tight hold on my waist and pulls me back towards him. He squeezes my hand until I cannot hold my grasp to his hair any longer.

"Will you ever listen? I warn you time and time again, but you never listen!"

He pushes me down again, my shoulder blades pushing down hard on the floor. Pulling a small, Black hand gun from the back of his pants, he begins to caress my face softly with it. The unwanted tears stream down my face.

"Please Daddy, don't do this.."

My voice is shaky, I know what happens when he sees me cry, and girls like me aren't allowed to cry.

"Shhh..It will all be over soon"

He runs the gun along the center of my chest, stopping just above the zipper of my pants, then pulls it away from me. Once he secures the gun back behind him, he brings his hands to my neck slowly, stroking my skin lovingly. I feel sick to my stomach. His large, rough hands wrap easily around my slender neck. Little by little, he applies pressure. Oh god, no no no!

His hands tighten around my neck, black specks obscure my vision along the edges. Soon, I will slip into unconsciousness, completely at his mercy. My father leans down towards my face, foam forming at the corners of his mouth when he harshly whispers,

"You are a whore just like your mother was. And you will die a whore's death like she did."

His grip tightens around my neck even more and I try to fight against the blackness. The full weight of his heavy body is resting directly on my chest making it difficult for me to move. I thrash my legs from side to side and grab onto his wrists around my neck, trying desperately to break free. It can't end like this, my life was finally coming together, I was finally starting to let go of my past.

Chapter Eighteen

My lungs fill with air in a rush, I start to cough uncontrollably. My eyes are still dark and blurred from the lack of oxygen and I feel weak and shaky. What the hell just happened? Hearing gasps and grunts coming from behind me, I turn around and see Jack and my father wrestling around on the floor.

I hadn't noticed Avery was here until she was kneeling down next to me, she must have come in here with Jack.

"Oh God! Morgan, are you okay?"

Avery helping me to my feet, Avery holds me steady as I stumble trying to right myself.

"Yeah, I...I think so".

Clasping my bruised, burning throat, I watch in horror as Jack tries desperately to keep my father down.

"Avery, you need to get out of here! Go get help now!"

"I can't leave you here Morgan! Oh my...Morgan..Your neck is beet red!"

"Avery you need to go now! I'm fine...I won't leave Jack! Please, please go."

I have to push Avery hard towards the door before she finally obeys. I make sure she is completely out of the apartment before I turn back around just as my father is shoving Jack in to the glass top table that sits in front of the couch.

Shards of glass shatter all around him as Jack's flailing body lands directly in the middle of the table. It was a sight of dismay when Jack's slow moving body rises up. Large chunks of glass are sticking out of his limbs, blood is flowing down the injured areas. My father takes quick strides towards Jack as he stands back up, but I make a mad dash for him. I jump on to my father's back, hanging on tight to his neck with one arm, while the other hand is ferociously clawing at his face. My father backs up close to the wall and shoves me in to it. The air

once again leaves my lungs, as I slide down the in a

daze.

Jack is up on his feet, grabbing my dad by the collar of

his shirt. He drags him to the opposite wall and throws

him up against it.

"Don't you dare touch her again!"

Jacks words come out in a loud growl, but my dad just

laughs and shakes his head, amused by Jack's

protectiveness.

"You stupid boy! You're going to try and defend

that little whore over there? Stupid, stupid, stupid. She

has corrupted you just like she has to all those other

boys."

Jack slams my dad up against the wall again, only much

harder this time.

Time stands still once again as Jack leaves my father and

slowly backs away from him to come for me. I watch as

my father reaches behind his back, and in that moment I

realize what's about to happen.

"Jack! Watch out! He has a gun!"

Jack whirls around to my father just as he pulls the trigger.

BANG

Utter silence once the shot rang. An anguished wince, a body swaying in place. Jack's eyes went wide with disbelief, a red stain flowed through the front of his shirt like the creek bed behind my old home. He looks down at it, then back at my father with puzzlement. Gravity takes hold of Jack. As gently as possible, I lean him back again the couch.

"Stay with me, Jack! Please baby, please"

The blood is pooling around the hole in his chest, just below his right shoulder. I apply pressure to it with on hand as I reach over to quickly open the desk drawer next to me. I dig around until I feel what I'm looking for. I pull out the one item of my father's that I had taken before fleeing Maine. I wanted something that would remind me of why I would never let that happen to me again. I grip on to the black handle and run my finger along the serrated edge of the blade. Turning towards my dad with no attention to spare, I lunge after him with the knife securely in the palm of my hand, blade out and ready. My father doesn't seem prepared for my fast approach.

I stop my approach just as I am toe to toe with him and raise the knife so he can see it.

"Remember this, Daddy?"

Not waiting for his response, I thrust the knife upwards as hard as I can in to the side of his throat.

My father stares at me with wide eyes, the shock of the impact evident on his face. He grips on to the handle of the knife and yanks it out, the knife making a clanking noise as it hits the floor. A gurgling sound comes from his mouth when he opens it to speak, blood is flowing from the deep gash on the side of his neck. I have to turn away from him. As much as I want to make sure he is truly dead this time, I just can't bring myself to watch him take his last breaths.

"Morgan?"

Jack mutters to himself. His eyes are closed and his hand is holding pressure to the gunshot. For a moment, I just look at him. He is still alive, and he had come back for me.

Kneeling down next to him, running my hand over his face, allowing him to feel my presence.

"I'm here, Jack. I'm here. It's all over."

He coughs and winces from the pain. His eyes shoot open quickly, but realizing it's me sitting next to him, he slowly closes them and relaxes. I look down at Jack, running my fingers along his shaven hair with my free hand.

"Jack, you need to stay with me...okay?...Avery went to get help, it's going to be alright soon".

Jack draws in a deep breath and lets it out, he places a

hand over mine,

"Morgan, I have to tell you this before I lose my nerve, having just been shot, I'm feel pretty ballsy".

He gives me a little smirk and tries to laugh it off, but you can see he is just as terrified as I am.

"Jack, stop. Once we get you fixed up, you can say whatever you need to say".

"No Morgan, I need to say this now. I love you Morgan...or Emma...or whatever you want to call yourself tomorrow. I love you."

I can't stop the tears that flow down my face. In the midst of what has happened today, I feel my soul soar at Jack's words. I believe them with all my heart, just like I believe what I'm going to tell him.

I lean down as softly as I can and whisper into his ear,

"I love you too, more than life itself."

Chapter Nineteen

I begged and pleaded with the Officer to let me go with Jack to the hospital but instead, I was put in to the back of the cop car with my hands securely cuffed in front of me. Before the officer completely shuts the door on me, I scream out to Avery who is sitting down, crying at the bottoms of the fire escape,

"Stay with Jack, Avery! Stay with him, do not leave his side!"

Avery nods her head at me, acknowledging what I just said and wraps her arms tight around herself and making her way to the ambulance. I watch until I see her getting into the back with Jack.

The sirens on the ambulance blare to life as they pull

away from the apartment building, holding the only man that I have ever truly loved and made me feel protected.

I try to cover my mouth to control my raging sobs, but once I see the second gurney emerge from the front door, I lose it even more. A black body bag rests on top of it, inside the remains of my father lay. I feel like I am back in the woods behind the house again, my hands and clothes are covered in his dried blood. The only real difference is that my father is truly dead this time.

The tan, stale brick walls felt like they were closing in on me, I'm not claustrophobic, but being stuck in this small room would certainly make anyone question their sanity. The air conditioner vent was wide open, blowing freezing cold air on to my bare-arms. Hours must have went by without anyone coming into the room to check on me, they were all most likely standing behind the two-way mirror wondering what kind of human-being they were going to encounter. If that is the case, they're going to get an honest one, I am tired of running and hiding, and I am finally ready to speak up. Jack is lying in a hospital, fighting for his life right now because of all the lies we lived in.

"Miss James?"

A tall, clean cut man wearing a white, crisp dress shirt and a blue striped tie walked in holding a clipboard and pen. Since I was going to be completely honest, I corrected the man as he sat down in the metal chair that is bolted to the ground across from me.

"Actually, my real name is Emma Reece. I called myself Morgan James once I got to San Francisco"

"Okay, Emma. I am going to be recording our conversation. I want you to answer any and all questions, if possible. Do you understand?"

"Yes Sir, I understand. I would also like to waive my right to a lawyer now, so we can get right to it, I am just so tired of it all"

"Let's begin then. What was your relationship with the deceased, Stanley Reece?"

Just hearing his name makes my stomach turn. I wipe the moisture pooling under my eyes,

"That Monster was my father"

Feeling safe enough to finally tell my story was more exhilarating than it was scary. No matter what happens to me after this, an ever crushing weight has been lifted off me by talking about it. I don't think the Detective was ready for my teenage tale, I think he had to stop me from finishing before I even had to stop myself. His fists would repeatedly clench as I retold all about my daily beating with the belt, never hitting hard enough to leave lasting marks and the threats of punishment by penetration, and finally the molestation itself. That was the hardest on him as I spared no detail, I needed him to know what It was like to be in my life and why I had to do what I did. Detective Lane excused himself from the interview several times in an attempt to keep his composure. After finishing the interview, Detective Lane left me alone in the room with promises of a change of clothes and food. I was relieved to be done talking for the time being.

A knock sounds on the interrogation room, the metal hinges of the steel door creak as it is pushed open. I am on my feet and racing into Miss Rose's arms before she even has a chance to speak.

"Oh Rose, What are you doing here and how did you even know I was here?"

Rose dabs the tears running down my cheek with a

kleenex she pulled from her gigantic purse.

"Avery called us, she thought you could use a familiar face since she was staying at the hospital with Jack"

"How is he, how is Jack?"

"Avery didn't have any updates since she wasn't a family member, but they did tell her that he was taken in to surgery immediately. Robert is on his way to the hospital to sit with Avery until his parents arrive. But how are you holding up, Dear?"

How could I even begin to explain to Rose how I was doing? I have a mixture of thoughts and feelings rushing through me all at once, I don't know where being scared begins and where relieved ends.

"I don't know, Rose. I just don't know much of anything right now except needing to make sure Jack is going to be okay. If he didn't show up when he did, I am positive

my father would have killed me"

Rose doesn't waste any time wrapping her arms around

me and softly smoothing down the back of my hair.

"Ohh Honey, We will figure this out together, you are

safe and no longer alone. That is all you need to think

about"

"I think I owe you and Robert both an explanation. For

all the lying I have done, I feel the worst about lying to

you and I am sincerely sorry for that"

"Shhhh, shhhh, Honey. From what little bit Avery told

us, you had good reason to keep the truth from

everyone. I just hope one day you are healed enough to

share your life with us. From the first time Robert and I

met you, we thought of you as one of our own"

A dam broke, I began to sob and shake uncontrollably.

Rose held me tight for several minutes while I let it all

out. I must have shed years of tears in those moments,

never once worrying about whether or not my father will catch me crying. It felt so good to let go.

Our moment was interrupted by Detective Lane and a woman in a black pencil skirt and matching blazer, who identified herself as the District Attorney.

"Miss Reece, In light of the circumstances and eye witnesses, we will not be pursuing charges at this time. This seems to be a clear case of self-defense and it seems to me that you and Mr. Sloan saved each other today"

Rose and I both hugged and cried with elated victory.

"Jack saved me not only today, but for the rest of my life"

Chapter Twenty

The news of my Father's passing and what he did to me

spread through my hometown, Oakler like wildfire. I

tried to shield my face as everyone walking along the

street stopped to stare at me. Jack sped the car up and

drove through town towards the house I thought I killed

my father in.

Stepping out of the sedan we rented at the airport, the

memories of my life came raging back to me. Jack

grabbed me by my waist just as I was falling to my knees. I couldn't hold back my sobs, I clutched my chest, feeling as if my heart was breaking in two. I hated my Father with a fiery passion, but what I hated more was I still felt a daughter's love for her father. After what he did to me, and finding out what he most certainly did to the Mother I never got to know, I should be spitting on his grave. Instead, I brought him home.

It had been five weeks before I made it back there with my Father's ashes. I was tempted to not claim the body that lay motionless in the morgue, but remembering how he was when I was a small child had me rethinking my temptations. Both Avery and Jack refused to let me do this on my own and I am thankful for that. I don't know what I would do without either of them by my side.

Jack holds me close against him, allowing me to weep for the loss of not just my Father, but my home, and the vanquishing of my demons as well. I wipe my eyes with the hem of my shirt, cursing myself for being so weak in this moment when I feel the need to be strong. Now is not the time to breakdown, now it the time to do what I came here to do and be gone.

"Morgan, do you want to look through any of the things in the house?"

"I don't know if I can."

Jack hugged me tighter against him, kissing me softly along my temple.

"We'll be right with you, if you want to go inside and look around."

"I have somewhere else I'd rather go. Would you both like to take a walk with me?"

In unison, Jack and Avery agreed to the walk.

The walk to Louis's cabin was much shorter than I remember it being, but the sense of ease that came over me the closer we came was undeniably calming. The trees that shadowed over the worn path seemed to have grown so much more. The limbs no longer looked like claws reaching out to snatch me up and bring me home, they still looked to be alive, but in a beautifully majestic way. The breeze carried the salted air from the coast across my face, bringing me back to the many times I came to Louis for comfort. Like years ago, Louis had a way of bringing peace to me, even when things were at their worst. Still, to this day, I never can understand what it was about him that made everything seem okay, that there truly is light at the end of the tunnel.

Jack laced his fingers through mine as we approached Louis's cabin, sensing my nervousness. I hadn't seen or spoken to Louis since the night of the fire and I wasn't sure if he has heard about my father's imminent death in San Francisco. Avery comes closer to my side, wrapping her arm around my waist, silently expressing her support if this visit didn't go well.

Looking up towards the small cabin, hidden within a

cluster of trees, I see the silhouette of a man that can only be Louis.

"Emma? Is that you? Is that really you?"

In that first moment of hearing his deep, grisly voice again, I sprint as fast as I can into is awaiting arms.

"Oh my. It is you! It is, it is. Hush now, it's alright now....Hush"

I hold Louis tight, never wanting to let go of the man that barely knew me and still opened his heart and home to me when I needed it. I held on to him and sobs until my tears ran completely dry.

"Oh Louis, I've missed you so much."

"Oh sweet Emma, I've missed you dearly. I'm so happy to see that you're okay."

I gestured to Jack and Avery to come forward. I needed them to meet that man that saved my sanity so many times over the years.

"Louis, I'd like you to meet Jack and Avery. Jack is,

well...I guess my boyfriend? We haven't really labeled ourselves...And Avery is my best friend...my sister. They both are very dear to me."

Louis gave Avery a soft smile, while giving her a gentle hug. Jack put out his hand to shake it, but Louis bypassed it and went in for another hug, obviously grateful to them both for being by my side.

"I cannot tell you both how happy it makes me to see Emma in such great hands."

Louis put his arm around my shoulders and guided us towards the water's edge where the waves were lapping, creating small swirls along the soft, warm sand.

"Louis, I don't think I can do this alone."

"I'm right here, my dear. I'm right here."

Louis held my hand and walked with me out into the cool water while Jack and Avery stayed behind.

Still holding Louis's hand tight, I lift the plain tin can up into the air, tilting it downward. I let the breeze catch the ashes, carrying them far out to sea. An instant sense of relief washed over me, all the fear and anger I had for my father lifted off my heavy shoulders, making me feel light and free.

"Will this pain in my heart ever go away?"

"My dear Emma, when you let people see your scars, you will begin to heal."

EPOLIGUE

Staring at the sign before me seemed unreal, after all
that had happened, I never thought this is how things
would turn out.

"Are you ready for this, Morgan?"

I link my hand with Jacks and stare into those
breathtaking eyes, loving how his left dimple comes out
to play when he gives me that sweet smirk of his.

"Today isn't just for me, it is for all of us. I can't believe the day is here, and we actually did it."

Before walking through the big blue double doors, Jack and I give the new sign another look.

M.J. GALLERY

I finally have my chance at being a real artist and being able to show others how to also, thanks to Rose and Robert.

After that last horrible night with my father, I refused to go back into that apartment. I couldn't stand the sight of Jack and my father's blood permanently stained into the floors. Rose and Robert opened their doors for Avery and I until we were able to find something we both felt comfortable in. After what had happened, I spent the majority of my time in the hospital, never leaving Jack's side and I never finished my canvases on time for the art gallery. George Froth was very understanding with everything that was going on, but he has a business to run and was unable to fit my work into his gallery in the near future. I strongly believed everything worked out the way it was supposed to. With me working in the book store and Jack recovering in the upstairs apartment Rose and Robert set up for us, the overflow of my completed canvases started getting noticed by customers and passerby's in the bookstore. Instead of asking about books, people started asking 'How much for the painting?'or 'Who is the artist?'. Robert came to me with an idea. He and Rose owned the small space next to the bookstore, but never knew what to do with it. I was to turn that space into a small gallery to show and sell my pieces, and in exchange I would pay a small rental fee for the space and still help out at the bookstore when needed. It was a dream come true for me, I didn't care if they had me working every day in the bookstore, just the chance to have a place to work and sell my pieces was enough to get me to agree with anything. I didn't want it to be just about me, I wanted to include the community as well. Much to my surprise, once I got the word out that I would give people the opportunity to learn to draw and paint, they were blowing up the answering machine to sign up.

Once Jack was up on his feet, he decided to look into a career change and do something he was always passionate about and went to college for, Photo Journalism. Once he got his photos out there, it didn't take long for him to get freelance work through smaller tourist magazines in the San Fran area. He still did a few investigative jobs here and there to bring in extra money, mostly the cheating husband or wife, but he has decided to stay away from the 'so-called runaways'. His parents, June and Tom were quite ecstatic when he shared the news with them. Jack had this amazing talent of capturing the true story whenever and wherever he was shooting for a magazine. I loved watching Jack work, you could see his eyes light up with joy and pride whenever he came home from a job to show me what he captured.

"Morgan, wait. This package came for you today, I thought you'd like to open before we went inside."

I let go of Jacks hand as Avery places, in my palms, a small package covered in brown paper bag wrapping, a small bow is tied at the top with straw–like yarn, holding it all together. Slowly untying the bow and pulling open the top, a hand woven seashell covered bracelet lay inside, a note beside it. Opening up the note, I smile at the sight of Louis's messy handwriting.

The note reads:

Take this bracelet and think of me often, as I will always think of you.

Tell Jack I said Yes.

Love your friend, Louis

Confusion was written all over my face when I turned to Jack as he is lowering down to the ground. Once my mind catches up to me, my breath hitches in my throat when realization hits me.

"Morgan, I have never loved another like I love you. I have Louis's blessing, now I ask for yours...will allow me to give you a blessed life by becoming my wife?"

There is no hesitation in my answer, there will never be hesitation or doubt where Jack is involved. My heart swells with such love and admiration for this man.

"Yes! Yes! I will!"

It's sometimes hard to believe that nearly two years ago, our lives were tilted on its axis, but today marks the day of new beginnings.

Today we start embarking on a new journey of welcoming a life of love, family, and healing, because once you have exposed the scars, you can let all the other good stuff in.

If you enjoyed Morgan's story, stay tuned for the whirlwind journey Avery is about to have.

Watch out for...

"Open Your Eyes"

www.ingramcontent.com/pod-product-compliance
Lightning Source LLC
Chambersburg PA
CBHW051425170626
46809CB00006B/2319